KU-362-694

Colonel Chabert

Honoré de Balzac

Translated by Andrew Brown

CLASS: F   BAL

No.   R 31363

AUTHOR | SUBJECT | DATE

1832 (2003)

6.95

apper 31

ET REMOTISSIMA PROPE

100 PAGES

100 PAGES

Published by Hesperus Press Limited
4 Rickett Street, London sw6 1ru
www.hesperuspress.com

First published in French in 1832
This translation first published by Hesperus Press Limited, 2003

Introduction and English language translation © Andrew Brown, 2003
Foreword © A.N. Wilson, 2003

Designed and typeset by Fraser Muggeridge
Printed in the United Arab Emirates by Oriental Press

isbn: 1-84391-037-3

All rights reserved. This book is sold subject to the condition that it shall not be
resold, lent, hired out or otherwise circulated without the express prior consent
of the publisher.

CONTENTS

FOREWORD

There are three categories of men in the Paris of the 1830s who habitually robed themselves in black: the Priest, the Doctor, and the Lawyer. Why?, asks Derville, the lawyer, at the end of this story; perhaps because they are in mourning for all the virtues and illusions lost by humanity. To this list of three must be added a fourth: the man who has the insight into human sin of the priest in the confessional, the forensic skill of a doctor dissecting human anatomy, the lawyer's vision of human fallibility and human greed. That fourth person is the novelist.

Balzac in some senses learnt what a novelist was, or could be, from reading Sir Walter Scott. In other senses he must be seen as purely original, a re-inventor of the novelist's role in history. He saw his fictions as a branch of science, every bit as revealing of life on the planet as those of the evolutionary biologists such as Lamarck who changed that generation's view of nature itself. Balzac's encyclopedic study of his own society – Parisian and provincial, public and private, rich and poor, high and low – was collectively a study of (to borrow the title of one of the greatest of his novels) Lost Illusions.

The novella *Colonel Chabert* was completed before any of Balzac's truly great novels were written, but only a year or two before two of his very best – *Eugenie Grandet* and *Père Goriot*. Already, we see in this short master-work a demonstration of Balzac's extraordinary abilities. From the teeming crowds of Paris, he plucks out now one individual, now another, and focuses his microscopic lens on their story. We discover that there are King Lears in common lodging-houses, Cleopatras in bordellos.

This particular story begins in a lawyer's office, with the clerks joking about the ragamuffin who keeps trying to gain an audience from their distinguished boss, Derville – a driven, work-obsessed figure who will crop up in about six of Balzac's other stories. Derville works all night in order to allow time for his social climbing and social observation. To this extent he may be seen not only as a portrait of a brilliant lawyer, but also as a paradigm of the novelist himself. For it is Derville's forensic skills which draw out the truth of the ragamuffin's story.

'*Notre vieux carrick*' – our old tramp in an outmoded form of overcoat – has come to Derville to establish his identity. He is in fact one Colonel Chabert, believed to have been killed on the Battlefield of Eylau, fighting for Napoleon. When Balzac wrote this story in 1832, the accession of Louis Philippe had led to an access of Napoleonic fervour once more in Paris, after the lacklustre Restoration monarchy. He could expect his readers to be moved by this old military hero, a Napoleonic man who was not an aristocrat but whose will-power and military skill had, by his own account, helped win one of the most important engagements in Eastern Prussia in 1814.

Colonel Chabert is believed dead, and his beautiful young wife, in this belief, has remarried a proper aristocrat, an ambitious thrusting young man who does not appear in the story but who stands a good chance of becoming a member of the House of Peers and a member of the government. As the Countess Ferraud, and the mother of two young aristocratic children, Chabert's wife (with his money) is enjoying a luxurious way of life, with a beautiful château and a small estate. Everything in her life appears to be that of an aristocrat of the old regime.

Chabert wants her back. He wants his money back. And the tension of the story at first consists in wondering whether, having persuaded Derville that he is not a confidence trickster, he will succeed in winning back his Rosine.

Derville has two marvellously evoked interviews with the Countess, in which he makes her admit that she had in fact received a letter from her supposedly dead husband before she married her new one. In other words, she knowingly committed bigamy. Derville persuades her that the best way out of the difficulty is a compromise, and the offer of some money to the old soldier. When Chabert and his wife actually meet, we half suppose that something in the nature of a reconciliation will occur between them, and that sentiment might begin to tug at our hearts.

The twist in the tale is that, outraged by her lack of sympathy and her meanness, Chabert throws back in her face the fact of her lowly social origins.

There are moments in the story when we almost think that the pair are going to behave decently towards one another – that, in exchange for being allowed a lodge on her grand estate, for example, Chabert will sink into anonymity and not claim his old name and inheritance. But he cooked his goose in an impulsive moment quite early on, by exclaiming, 'I picked you up at the Palais-Royal...' ('*Je vous ai prise au Palais-Royal*'). Looking back on the whole story, Derville recalls the tiger-expression which the Countess cast her ex-husband when he made the recollection that he 'taken' her, as one might pick up a cab in a public place. The French word '*prendre*' can mean as many things as the English word 'take'; it ranges from purchase to physical possession. It is hardly the language of love.

The borderline between prostitution and marriage – and indeed the borderline between prostitution and all other human relationships – the advantages which men and women exploit in one another, the knowledge that money can buy anything and that money is power, this guilty knowledge informs the whole of Balzac's view of society and of human nature. Chabert, the old war hero, lives out his days in a pauper's hostel. The woman who was just a bit of baggage picked up off the street ends by being a high aristocrat, and almost too pious. Yet we might equally note that Chabert's attitude to her had been possessive and patronising, and conclude that she is exacting a perfectly appropriate revenge. Balzac is not a heavy moralist, but he shows, as in some demonstration in a scientific laboratory, the inevitable workings of human beings upon one another.

In the final dialogue, Godeschal, Derville's colleague, says that he has suddenly been taken ill – struck with the malady of disgust with humanity. Reading Balzac is not a reassuring experience. It challenges our humanism, if we have any, but it ultimately does not destroy it. To the lawyer's sense of human corruption, the doctor's dissecting skill, and the priest's ear in the confessional, he adds the ingredient without which no fiction can really function: a knowledge of the human heart, which, however jaded and disgusted it may feel, is born of sympathy.

– A.N. Wilson, 2003

At the end of January 1807, Napoleon and his *Grande Armée* chased the Russian Army through the blizzards of a wintry East Prussia. In an anticipation of the great campaign of 1812, when Napoleon marched into Russia itself, the Russians had two things in their favour: firstly, their ability to retreat at the right moment, luring the French ever onwards into the eastern immensities from which so many of them would never return; and secondly, General Winter. In 1807 Napoleon was aiming at Königsberg, where the Prussian King Friedrich Wilhelm III had established his temporary capital; the Russians halted to block his path, taking up position near the town of Preussisch-Eylau. The Battle of Eylau, fought under a heavy fall of snow on 8 February 1807 between two rows of frozen lakes, set 80,000 Russians against about 60,000 French. The French infantry, subjected to heavy Russian cannonades, fell back in disarray; Davout and Ney did not bring their French troops into action until it was almost too late. What saved the *Grande Armée* from complete defeat, ensuring that the battle was no worse than a particularly ruinous draw, were the French cavalry charges repeatedly launched straight at the centre of the Russian and Prussian lines. One of these charges was led by Colonel Chabert: the troops under his command broke through the Russian lines, but as they tried to return to their own side, Chabert himself was cut down from his horse by a Russian sabre, and disappeared under the hooves of the 1500-strong cavalry charge led by Murat. Napoleon, who held Chabert in high esteem and was later to declare that the Colonel had saved the day for him, sent surgeons to discover whether his life could be saved; but they found what they took to be a lifeless body, and he was later buried in the common grave of those slain on the battlefield – of whom there were many, for nearly a third of the French troops had been killed or wounded in the engagement. When Ney surveyed the battlefield the following day, he exclaimed, 'What a massacre, and without result!' This did not prevent Napoleon sending news of his inevitable 'victory' back to Paris, whereupon he set about retreating with his starving army, through temperatures of minus twenty-two degrees, to winter quarters. Vexed at his failure to take Königsberg, he declared that such had never been his intention in the first place.

'The grapes would have been sour anyway,' said the fox, and trotted away. Those who take part in historic events are just as inventive at editing their motives and memories as the historians who try to find out, in the words of the German historian Ranke, '*wie es eigentlich gewesen*', what it was really like, or the novelists who try to re-imagine historical experience in more intimate ways. So much fact, so much fiction. The Battle of Eylau took place: at least, a huge sequence of events has been subsumed, for the sake of intelligibility, under that name, which, like all names ('Napoleon', 'Chabert'), is a useful kind of shorthand. I have taken the details of the battle from a recent history of Napoleon's campaigns, but I added one item not to be found in any historical account, though it is found in Balzac's story: the cavalry charge led by Colonel Chabert. Although he is what the French call '*vraisemblable*', a perfectly plausible figure, he did not exist as such, and his name is not (despite his claims) signalled in the list of *Victories and Conquests*. Likewise, the history books do not refer to the presence of a Prince Andrei Bolkonsky fighting for the Russians at Austerlitz (as Tolstoy depicts him in *War and Peace*), or a Fabrice del Dongo at Waterloo (as in Stendhal's *The Charterhouse of Parma*). But once you have read Balzac,

Tolstoy, or Stendhal, it is difficult to peruse historical accounts of Napoleonic battles without the field being haunted by their fictitious protagonists, just as their fictions are haunted by our awareness of history (we know, as we read *War and Peace*, that Napoleon will be defeated: if this were not the case, the novel would not exist in the first place). What we read first (history through fiction, or fiction through history) matters: it's a question of precedence – like the question of who is Countess Ferraud's real husband: her first husband, Chabert, whom she believed to have died at Eylau; or her second husband, Count Ferraud.

Colonel Chabert is a story of hauntings. The fictitious Chabert, as we learn early on, did not perish at Eylau but was buried alive, and managed to escape from the common grave, emerging as naked as from his mother's womb. The symbolic and mythical dimensions of the story are powerfully suggested: his survival is a rebirth, or even a resurrection. But it gives little cause for joy. The Napoleon he had served, that tyrant of genius (in every sense of the phrase) for whom he maintains a sentimental devotion, is now on St Helena, having himself staged a rebirth (the escape from exile on Elba) that led merely to renewed defeat and definitive exile. And when Chabert returns to France, he discovers that he is no longer wanted, either by his wife, or by his country, both of them having, as it were, changed regime: his wife by remarrying, his country (his 'fatherland', he calls it) by accepting as its master after Napoleon's fall the restored Bourbon Louis XVIII. The history of France in the nineteenth century is indeed a history of repetitions and comebacks, or '*revenants*' (the French word for ghosts means 'those who return'). History itself can be spookily recursive, caught in a time warp, endlessly recycling old systems of government and outdated regimes. The French

Revolution that began in 1789 swept from power an absolutist monarch, Louis XVI, and was followed by the First Republic, then the Directory and Empire under a Napoleon who ended up as yet another absolutist monarch; he was defeated and exiled, but returned, only to be defeated and exiled again. He was succeeded by the restored monarchy of Louis XVIII, who had returned from exile in 1814, fled from Paris in 1815 during the Hundred Days, and returned again after Waterloo. Then came the autocracy of Charles X who hoped to return France to the days of the *Ancien Régime*, was exiled at the revolution of 1830 and succeeded by the 'bourgeois' monarchy of Louis-Philippe, who was exiled after the revolution of 1848 and succeeded by the Second Republic, which succumbed to the *coup d'état* of the previously exiled Louis Napoleon (nephew of Napoleon I) in 1851 and the Second Empire, which collapsed during the Franco-Prussian War to be replaced by the Third Republic in 1870, with Louis Napoleon in turn taking the road into exile... So many comings and goings of kings and emperors, so many exiles returning to assume or reassume power before departing into exile again: every monarch haunted by Napoleon (haunted by the desire to be him, or to prevent anyone like him ever rising to seize power again), every revolution haunted by the Revolution (haunted by the desire to live up to it, or to correct its errors).

Marx claimed how much he had learnt about the socio-political history of France from Balzac. One of the things he learnt was the power of the symbol. The famous first sentence of the Communist Manifesto could justifiably be rewritten: 'A spectre is haunting history – the spectre of the symbol'. Louis Napoleon, obsessed by the imperial glory of his uncle, tried to reincarnate that symbol in a France that finally and belatedly moved on. Chabert, having 'died' and been resurrected, returns to a reality in which he can no longer find a place, but where his very presence is seen as an embarrassment and a threat. He symbolises all that the new France refuses to acknowledge: Napoleon, military heroism, and above all the ever-present possibility that the past never achieves closure, but lingers on – in short, the symbol. He is like a Vietnam vet haunting the America of the years after 1973. The harshness shown by Countess Ferraud to her first husband is no greater than that of a whole society, which seems to have condemned other survivors of the *Grande Armée* – Chabert's old comrade Vergniaud, for instance, now a humble dairyman living in squalor in one of the most sordid of Paris suburbs – to an equally shameful 'posthumous' existence. Countess Ferraud herself is a Penelope who has rewoven the web of her life story to edit out her missing Odysseus rather than, as in Homer, to stave off any successor; but the story does not condemn her for her 'unfaithfulness'. She is indeed cruel towards Chabert, but her choices are circumscribed: if she does not have him locked away, she will always be vulnerable to the loss of her own new identity as a wife and mother. She is also haunted, as a woman with little real political power of her own, by the fear that her second husband, Count Ferraud, will find her too socially unconnected for his own political ambitions and divorce her so as to pick up a peerage (a divorce that Chabert's return and the disclosure of her own bigamy would make easier). Given the restless flux of history, it is easy to understand why Balzac's characters might fight tooth and nail for something enduring – once, that is, they have used those very same historical vicissitudes to get their hands on it in the first place. In presenting us with a clash between two claims for identity, Chabert's and Countess Ferraud's, which in the prevailing social conditions cannot be synthesised,

Balzac has produced not just another jeremiad about the self-seeking egotism of contemporary society, but a tragedy.

Still, the focus remains on Chabert. His own people 'receive him not', and his society has changed to the point of unrecognisability: his old house has been knocked down to make way for new housing; he left France a post-Revolutionary Empire and returns to find it practically a pre-Revolutionary monarchy; he left a childless Countess Chabert and returns to find a Countess Ferraud with two children. The old order had been based on names, the new order is based on money. Just as Marx may have learnt something about the power of the symbol in Balzac, he certainly found confirmation of his own views on economics: Balzac acted as Virgil guiding Marx's Dante through the infernal labyrinth of France's nascent capitalism. Money had replaced land (the huge swathes of France owned by the aristocracy before the Revolution) as an index of status. Though *Colonel Chabert* is set in the reign of Louis XVIII, Balzac wrote it under Louis-Philippe, who presided over a period of industrial expansion and financial boom, and the volatile somersaults of the market dominate Balzac's entire oeuvre. A fine short essay on *Colonel Chabert* by Laura Villon, in the arts review of the *World Socialist* website (see details in the 'Note on the Text', below), gives a succinct *marxisant* summary of the way Chabert, 'a man of honour', falls victim to the new money-grubbing France of the post-Napoleonic era. In this society, money is the most real of all things, but Marx also points out how abstract money is – it can be exchanged for anything, and so has no real identity of its own; it is here one minute, and gone the next (at the spin of a wheel of the gambling table, or – what amounts to the same thing – the rise or fall of share prices on the Bourse); its numbers can grant or withhold the prestige previously associated with, for instance, a good family name. So *Colonel Chabert* begins with a scribe in a lawyer's office totting up a bill, and it ends with Chabert in the old folks' home, declaring that he is no longer a name, but a number.

Balzac shows two ways of reacting to this society of merciless rapacity, status-seeking, and ingratitude. Derville, the decent lawyer who has done his best to restore Chabert to his position, ends the narrative with a list of examples of the mercenary heartlessness so endemic in his society (they are all taken from Balzac's other novels); faced with such incorrigible turpitude, he is happy to retire with his wife from the battlefield of Paris to the countryside. This withdrawal is one shared by many of the morally most appealing characters in Balzac's world, but it condemns itself to a washing of the hands in the face of the world's iniquity, and to a politics of quietistic resignation. Far more interesting is the renunciation of Chabert. The winning card played by his wife in her struggle against him is that of her children. Chabert, impelled by nausea at his wife's turpitude, nostalgia for Napoleon, and emotion at the sight of her children, decides that he must die again, as he had once done on the field of Eylau: he must allow his society to bury him alive as Napoleon's careless surgeons had tossed him into the common grave. His relinquishing of the struggle against his wife's refusal to acknowledge him is a symbolic death. But old soldiers do not die, they just fade away; indeed, Chabert does not even simply fade away, he metamorphoses into a new state of being, 'an old philosopher full of imagination', maybe even 'happy': a 'poem' or a 'drama', like the beggars in the streets of our world ('spare us any change,' they say, ambiguously: a question or an imperative?). He will no longer be Chabert, but at best 'Hyacinthe', a name with nicely mythical resonances. He has abandoned the search to be recognised by his society; this may mean that, like Derville, he is impotent to change it, but whereas there is something regressive in Derville's resignation, there is something revolutionary in Chabert's renunciation, amounting as it does to a critique of all the mechanisms of naming and recognition. Why allow the state, whether Napoleonic or Bourbon, to dictate the terms of one's identity, with its names and titles? Why try to extort, from the morally bankrupt institutions of a bourgeois civil society so obviously devoid of all legitimacy, a recognition of who you are that can only ever be a miscognition? Why keep trying to get it to return your name and fortune to you? Why keep trying, yourself, to return? There are children, and the future; and however much history is in thrall to repetition, there is always the hope that the curse under which it labours (the eternal return of the same) will be broken. As so often, a great realist novelist has produced a profoundly symbolic story: Chabert in his dotage anticipates the evolving forms of subjectivity we find in Beckett's increasingly anonymous characters, all those Molloys, Malones and other Unnameables, deprived of (or emancipated from) the trammels of an identity that, in a false society, can only ever be that of an impostor. Free of such impositions, Chabert accepts that even the happiest returns of the day are of little significance when compared to what has been called, in terms of grave provocation, the resurrection of the dead and the life of the world to come.

– *Andrew Brown, 2003*

Note on the Text:

This translation is based on *Colonel Chabert*, edited by Stéphane Vachon (Paris: Librairie générale française, 'Le Livre de Poche classique', 1994). The work on Napoleon's campaigns whose account of the Battle of Eylau I summarise is the volume by Correlli Barnett in the 'Wordsworth Military Library' series: Bonaparte (Ware, Herts, Wordsworth Editions Ltd, 1997, first published 1978). The article by Laura Villon can be found on the website published by the International Committee of the Fourth International: www.wsws.org (29 May 2000).

Colonel Chabert

'Ah! Our old greatcoat again!'

Such was the exclamation that fell from the lips of a clerk belonging to the type known in law firms as 'errand-boys', who at this moment was biting with a very hearty appetite into a hunk of bread; he pulled off a bit of the crust to roll it into a little pellet and flick it mockingly through the opening of a window he was leaning against. The pellet, unerringly aimed, rebounded almost back up to the level of the casement, after striking the hat of a stranger who was walking across the courtyard of a house on the rue Vivienne, where lived Monsieur Derville, solicitor.

'Hey, Simonnin, stop messing around with people or I'll throw you out. However poor a client may be, he's still a man, for heaven's sake!' said the chief clerk, stopping in the middle of totting up the bill for a memorandum of costs.

The errand-boy is generally, as was Simonnin, a boy of thirteen to fourteen years old, who in every law firm is under the special dominion of the chief clerk whose little odd jobs and love letters keep him busy even when he is taking writs to bailiffs and requests for a hearing to the lawcourts. In his way of life he resembles a streetwise Parisian lad, and in his destiny he belongs to the tribe of pettifogging lawyers. He is a boy almost always devoid of pity, unchecked, uncontrollable, quick with his tongue, jeering, avid and lazy. Still, almost every junior clerk has, living in some dingy room up on the fifth floor, an old mother with whom he shares the thirty or forty francs allocated to him per month.

'If he's a man, why do you call him "old greatcoat"?' said Simonnin, with the expression of a schoolboy catching his teacher out.

And he went back to eating his bread and cheese, leaning his shoulder against the stile of the window, since he took his rest standing up, like the cab-horses of Paris, with one of his legs bent and propped on his other shoe's toe.

'Think of the fun we could have with that old codger!' muttered the third clerk, Godeschal by name, as he paused in the middle of a line of argument he was developing in a petition to be copied out in a fair hand by the fourth clerk, the draft copies of which were made by two novices fresh from the provinces. Then he continued with his improvisation: '... But, in his noble and benevolent wisdom, His Majesty Louis The Eighteenth (spell it out in full, now, won't you, Desroches you wise old thing, when you make the fair copy!), at the moment when he took up once more the reins of his Kingdom, understood... (what did that old clown ever understand?) the lofty mission to which he was summoned by Divine Providence! ...... (exclamation mark for admiration, followed by six dots: they're devout enough in the lawcourts to let us have that many), and his first thought was, as witness the date of the below-mentioned ordinance, to repair the misfortunes caused by the terrible and lamentable disasters of our revolutionary period, by granting restitution to his faithful and numerous servants ("numerous" is a piece of flattery that should go down well with the lawcourts) all their unsold goods, whether they were in the public domain, whether they were in the ordinary or extraordinary domain of the Crown, or whether, finally, they were in endowments given to public establishments, for we are and consider ourselves competent to maintain that such is the spirit and the letter of the celebrated and most loyal ordinance delivered in... – Wait a minute,' said Godeschal to the three clerks, 'this wretched sentence has gone on right to the end of my page. – Well anyway,' he continued, wetting with his tongue the back fold of the sheet so he could turn the thick page of its stamped paper, 'well anyway, if you want to play a trick on him, just tell him that the boss can only speak to his clients between two and three o'clock in the morning: we'll see if the old rogue turns up!' And Godeschal went back to the sentence he had started: 'Delivered in… Got it?' he asked.

'Got it!' shouted the three copyists.

Everything proceeded simultaneously – petition, conversation and conspiracy.

'Delivered in… Hey, Boucard old friend, what's the date of the ordinance? We have to make sure all our *i*'s are dotted, for Christ sakes! That adds a few pages.'

'For Christ sakes!' repeated one of the copyists before Boucard, the chief clerk, could reply.

'What, you've written "For Christ sakes"?' exclaimed Godeschal, peering at one of the newcomers with eyes that were at once severe and roguish.

'Oh yes,' said Desroches, the fourth clerk, leaning over to look at his neighbour's copy, 'he's written: "We have to make sure all our *i*'s are dotted", and "ferchrissakes" as one word.'

All the clerks burst out laughing.

'So, Monsieur Huré, you think "for Christ sakes" is a legal term, and you claim to be from Mortagne!' exclaimed Simonnin.

'Scratch that out!' said the chief clerk. 'If the judge appointed to fix costs in the case could see such things, he'd say someone was taking the mickey! You'd cause the boss real hassle. Come on, stop messing about, Monsieur Huré! Someone from Normandy shouldn't write a petition without due care and attention. It's the "Shoulder arms!" of m'learned friends.'

'Delivered in… in?…' asked Godeschal. 'Go on, when was it, Boucard?'

'June 1814,' replied the first clerk, without pausing in his own work.

A knock at the door of the office interrupted the sentence in the prolix petition. Five clerks, all blessed with hearty appetites, alert and mocking eyes, and fine heads of hair, lifted their noses from their work and turned to the door, after all chorusing at once: 'Come in!' Boucard remained with his face buried in a pile of papers, called red tape in the style of the lawcourts, and continued composing the memo of costs he was working on.

The office was a spacious room adorned with the classic stove that embellishes all the dens of pettifoggery. Its pipes crossed the chamber diagonally and converged on a blocked-up mantelpiece on whose marble top could be seen various scraps of bread, triangles of Brie, fresh pork cutlets, glasses, bottles, and the chief clerk's cup of drinking chocolate. The odour of these foodstuffs blended so well with the stench of the excessively overheated stove, and with the smell charac-teristic of offices and bundles of paperwork, that the stink of a fox would have passed unnoticed in it. The floor was already covered with the mud and snow traipsed in by the clerks. Near the window stood the chief clerk's cylindrical writing-desk, and right up against it was the little table for the use of the second clerk. The latter was at this particular moment at the lawcourts. It was maybe eight or nine o'clock in the morning. The only decoration in the office was those big yellow posters announcing distraint of goods, sales, auctions between majors and minors, definitive or preparatory adjudications: all the power and glory of law firms! Behind the chief clerk was a huge set of pigeon-holes, filling the wall from top to bottom, each of them stuffed with bundles of paper from which there dangled countless labels and wisps of red thread of the sort that give a special appearance to the documents involved in legal proceedings. The lower rows of pigeon-holes were full of cardboard boxes yellowed by long use, and fringed with blue paper: on them could be read the names of the big clients whose juicy bits of business were being concocted at this very moment. The dirty window-panes allowed little light to trickle through. In any case, in February there are very few offices where you can write without the help of a lamp before ten o'clock in the morning, for all such offices are, as you might expect, quite neglected: everyone goes there but nobody stays, and no personal interest can attach to such a humdrum place; neither the solicitor, nor the litigants, nor the clerks can be bothered to maintain the elegance of a spot which for some is a classroom, for others a passage, and for the master a laboratory. The filthy furniture is handed down from solicitor to solicitor with such religious scruple that certain offices still possess boxes of amounts still owing, moulds for parchment latchets, bags that originated with the lawyers at the 'Chlet', the abbreviated form of the word CHATELET, a jurisdiction which represented in a bygone order of things the present-day Court of First Hearing[1]. So this dingy office, greasy with dust, was, like all the others, quite repellent for litigants, and its dismal appearance made it one of the most monstrously hideous places in Paris. Indeed, if the damp sacristies where prayers are weighed and paid for like spices, and if the second-hand clothes shops where we see rags trailing around as a proof of the futility of all our illusions and a demonstration of where all our partying leads us – if these two cesspools of poetry did not exist, a solicitor's office would be of all social emporia the most horrible. But the same is true of gambling dens, lawcourts, lottery kiosks and places of ill repute. Why? Perhaps in these places the drama which unfolds in a man's soul makes his appurtenances seem a matter of indifference to him: and this would explain the single-mindedness of great thinkers and those who nurse great ambitions.

'Where's my penknife?'

'I'm having my breakfast!'

'Oh, just sod off, I've blotted my petition!'

'Shhhh, gentlemen!'

These various exclamations were all rattled off simultaneously at the moment the old litigant closed the door with the kind of humility which puts a crimp in the movements of every unhappy man. The stranger tried to sketch a smile, but the muscles in his face fell back into place once he had sought in vain any symptoms of affability on the inexorably apathetic faces of the six clerks. No doubt accustomed to weighing up men at first glance, he addressed himself with considerable politeness to the errand-boy, in the hope that this drudge would give him a mild and gentle answer.

'Monsieur, can your superior be seen now?'

For all reply to the poor man, the malicious errand-boy merely tapped his ear repeatedly with the fingers of his left hand, as if to say: 'I'm deaf.'

'What do you want, Monsieur?' asked Godeschal, whose question emerged from a mouth munching a hunk of bread big enough to load a cannon with, as he brandished his knife and crossed his legs so that the foot that was up in the air came level with his eyes.

'This is the fifth time I have come here, Monsieur,' replied the suppliant. 'I wish to speak to Monsieur Derville.'

'Is it on business?'

'Yes, but I can explain it only to Monsieur…'

'The boss is asleep. If you want to consult him about a particular problem, he only really works at midnight. But if you could tell us about your case, we could maybe be of just as much assistance as him…'

The stranger remained impassive. He started to look modestly around, like a dog who, slipping into a kitchen where he should not be, fears he might be kicked out. By the grace attaching to their estate, clerks are never frightened by the prospect of thieves, and so these particular clerks harboured no suspicions regarding the man in the greatcoat, and allowed him to inspect their office, where he looked in vain for a chair on which to rest, for he was visibly tired. Solicitors leave few chairs around in their offices, out of principle. The common-or-garden client, weary of having to stand, goes off grumbling, but at least he doesn't take up a time that, in the words of an old lawyer, can't be claimed *on expenses.*

'Monsieur,' he replied, 'I have already had the honour of informing you that I can explain my business only to Monsieur Derville, and so I will wait for him to get up.'

Boucard had finished adding up his bill. He smelled the odour wafting from his chocolate, rose from his wickerwork chair, crossed to the mantelpiece, looked the old man up and down, stared at the greatcoat, and pulled an indescribable face. He probably thought that, however much they squeezed this client, it would be impossible to extract a single centime from him; then he intervened with a few brief remarks intended to rid of the office of a waste of space.

'They're telling you the whole truth, Monsieur. The boss works only at night-time. If your business is serious, I recommend you return at one o'clock in the morning.'

The client looked at the chief clerk with a stupid expression on his face, and remained motionless for a few moments. The clerks, used to every change in people's physiognomies and the strange whims produced by the indecision or day-dreaming characteristic of the whole brood of litigants, carried on eating, making as much noise with the chomping of their jaws as horses doubtless make at their rack, and took no more notice of the old man.

'Monsieur, I will come this evening,' the old fellow finally said: with the tenacity peculiar to unhappy people, he wanted to show up humanity's failings.

The only epigram permitted to Wretchedness is that of forcing Justice and Charity to reject them without just cause. When the unhappy have convicted Society of lying, they are all the more eager to throw themselves into the arms of God.

'My, isn't he a *bold* one?' said Simonnin, without waiting for the old man to have closed the door behind him.

'Looks like a corpse they dug up,' replied the junior clerk.

'He's some colonel or other, chasing his arrears,' said the chief clerk.

'No, he's a retired concierge,' said Godeschal.

'Bet you he's a noble,' exclaimed Boucard.

'No, *I* bet he was a porter,' replied Godeschal. 'Porters are the only ones to be endowed by Nature with worn-out, greasy greatcoats all tattered and torn at the edges like the one the old chap was wearing! Didn't you even see his leaky, down-at-heel boots, or his cravat doing service as a shirt? He knows what it is to sleep under bridges.'

'He could be a noble who's spent time as a doorman,' exclaimed Desroches. 'It's been known to happen!'

'No,' replied Boucard, amid the ensuing laughter, 'what I think is that he was a brewer in 1789, and a colonel under the Republic.'

'Aha! I'll buy everyone here a ticket to see a show if it turns out he was ever a soldier,' said Godeschal.

'You're on,' replied Boucard.

'Monsieur! Monsieur?' shouted the junior clerk, opening the window.

'What are you doing, Simonnin?' asked Boucard.

'I'm calling him to ask if he's a colonel or a porter – after all, if anyone knows, *he* does!'

All the clerks burst out laughing. As for the old man, he was already coming back up the stairs.

'What'll we tell him?' exclaimed Godeschal.

'Leave it to me!' replied Boucard.

The poor man came timidly back in, his eyes downcast, perhaps so as not to reveal how hungry he was by gazing too avidly at all the food.

'Monsieur,' said Boucard to him, 'would you be so kind as to give us your name, so that the boss can know if…'

'Chabert.'

'You mean the colonel who died at Eylau?' asked Huré – he hadn't said anything yet and was jealously waiting for a chance to add his pennyworth of wit to all the others.

'The same, Monsieur,' replied the old fellow, with a classical simplicity. And he withdrew.

'Gosh!'

'Sacked!'

'Pop!'

'Oh!'

'Ah!'

'Vavoom!'

'The old clown!'

'Dum dee dum dee dum!'

'Gotcha!'

'Monsieur Desroches, you've won a free trip to see a show,'

said Huré to the fourth clerk, slapping him on the back so heartily he would have killed a rhinoceros.

A torrent of laughter, shouts and exclamations poured out: if we tried to depict it, we would use up all the onomatopoeias in the language.

'Which theatre shall we go to?'

'The Opera!' cried the chief.

'To begin with,' replied Godeschal, 'I didn't say *theatre*. If I want, I can take you to see Madame Saqui[2].'

'Madame Saqui is not a show,' said Desroches.

'And what exactly is a show?' answered Godeschal. 'We should first establish the *facts of the matter*. What did I wager, gentlemen? A show. What is a show? Something you go and see…'

'But on that basis I suppose you could keep your promise by taking us to see the water flowing under the Pont-Neuf!' Simonnin broke in.

'You have to pay good money to see it,' continued Godeschal.[3]

'But you have to pay good money to see all sorts of things that aren't a show. The definition is not precise,' said Desroches.

'Let me have my say!'

'You're talking nonsense, my friend,' said Boucard.

'Is Curtius a show?' said Godeschal.

'No,' replied the chief clerk. 'It's a waxworks.'

'I bet a hundred francs to one sou,' continued Godeschal, 'that Curtius' waxworks constitute the collection of objects upon which the name "show" has devolved. It consists of something to be seen for different prices, depending on where you want to sit…'

'And Bob's your uncle,' said Simonnin.

'You watch it if you don't want a smack in the face!' said Godeschal.

The clerks shrugged.

'Anyway, there's nothing to prove that the old baboon wasn't taking us for a ride,' he said, abandoning his argument that had been drowned out by the laughter of the other clerks. 'In all conscience, Colonel Chabert is well and truly dead, his wife remarried Count Ferraud, of the Council of State. Madame Ferraud is one of our clients!'

'The case is held over until tomorrow,' said Boucard. 'To work, gentlemen! Hang it all! Nobody's doing a tap of work here. Get your petition finished, it's got to be notified before the session in the fourth Chamber. The case is being judged today. Gee up!'

'If it *had* been Colonel Chabert, wouldn't he have stuck the toe of his boot up the backside of that fool of a Simonnin when he pretended to be deaf?' said Desroches, viewing this observation as more conclusive than that of Godeschal.

'Since nothing is decided,' continued Boucard, 'let's agree to get tickets for the upper circle at the Français to see Talma playing Nero[4]. Simonnin can go in the stalls.'

Upon which, the chief clerk sat down at his desk, and everyone did likewise.

'Delivered in June eighteen hundred and fourteen (spell it out),' said Godeschal, 'got it?'

'Yes,' replied the two draft copyists and the fair-hand copyist, as their quills began to scratch their way again across the stamped paper, filling the office with the noise of a hundred cockchafers caught by schoolboys and kept in paper cornets.

'And we hope that the Gentlemen composing the Court,' improvised Godeschal. 'Hang on! I've got to reread my sentence, I've lost the thread of my thoughts.'

'Forty-six... That must happen a lot!... And three makes forty-nine,' said Boucard.

'We hope,' resumed Godeschal, after reading his work through, 'that the Gentlemen composing the Court will be no less great than is the august author of the ordinance, and that they will treat with the requisite severity the contemptible claims of the administration of the Grand Chancellery of the Legion of Honour, firmly establishing the jurisprudential arrangements in the broad sense we are here setting forth...'

'Monsieur Godeschal, would you like a glass of water?' said the junior clerk.

'You clown, Simonnin!' said Boucard. 'Here, saddle your trusty steed, take this packet and gallop over to the Invalides as quick as you can.'

'...we are here setting forth,' resumed Godeschal. 'Add: in the interest of Madame (spell it out) the Vicomtesse de Grandlieu...'

'What's that?' exclaimed the chief clerk, 'you're taking it into your head to draw up petitions in the case "Vicomtesse de Grandlieu versus Legion of Honour", a case that's been left hanging around the office, a piece of contract work? You ninny! Will you please put your copies and your memo to one side, you can keep it for the case "Navarreins versus the Hospices". It's getting late, I'm going to do a bit of work on a request for a hearing, with all the whys and the wherefores, and I'll go to the lawcourts myself...'

This scene represents one of the thousand pleasures that, in later life, make people say, as they look back at their youth: 'Ah, those were the days!'

At about one o'clock in the morning, the self-styled Colonel Chabert came and knocked on the door of Monsieur Derville, solicitor of the Court of First Hearing of the *département* of the Seine. The porter told him that Monsieur Derville was not home yet. The old man replied that he had an appointment and went up the stairs to see this celebrated lawyer who, in spite of his youth, had the reputation of being one of the best legal brains in the lawcourts. After ringing the bell, the mistrustful suppliant was no little astonished to see the first clerk busy setting out on his employer's dining-room table the numerous files of the different cases coming up the next day, and putting them in the right order. The clerk, just as astonished, greeted the Colonel and asked him to take a seat; this the suitor did.

'Good lord, Monsieur, I thought you must be joking yesterday when you told me to come so very early in the morning for a consultation,' said the old fellow, with the false jocularity of a ruined man who is forcing himself to smile.

'The clerks were joking and telling the truth at the same time,' said the principal clerk, as he continued his work. 'Monsieur Derville has chosen this time to examine his cases, summarise their grounds put forward, order their conduct, and arrange their pleas. His powerful intelligence feels more free at this hour, as it's the only time he can enjoy the silence and tranquillity necessary to hatch good ideas. Since he has been a solicitor, you are the third example of a consultation given at this nocturnal hour. Once he's back home, the boss will think over every case, read everything, spend maybe four or five hours working, then he will ring for me and explain his intentions. In the mornings, between ten and two o'clock, he hears his clients, then he uses the rest of the day to make his visits. In the evenings, he goes out into the world to see his friends and acquaintances. So that just leaves the night for him to ponder his forthcoming trials, ransack the arsenals of the

Civil Code, and lay his battle plans. He doesn't want to lose a single case; he loves his art. He won't take on just any old case, as his colleagues do. That's his life – an extraordinarily active life. That's why he earns so much money.'

As he listened to this explanation, the old man remained silent, and his bizarre face assumed an expression so devoid of intelligence that the clerk, after scrutinising him, paid him no further attention. A few moments later, Derville came back, wearing evening dress; his chief clerk opened the door for him, and went back to finish arranging the files. The young solicitor stood for a moment gazing dumbstruck as he caught sight of the singular client waiting for him in the dim half-light. Colonel Chabert was as completely motionless as a waxwork figure in the Curtius museum to which Godeschal had wanted to take his friends. This immobility would not perhaps have been a cause for astonishment were it not for the fact that it added the final touch to the supernatural spectacle presented by the personage as a whole. The old soldier was thin and lean. His forehead, deliberately concealed beneath the hair of his smooth wig, created an impression of mystery. His eyes seemed to be covered with a transparent veil: they looked like dirty mother-of-pearl, with their blueish reflections shining tremulously in the light of the candles. His pale, livid 'hatchet face', if we may use that common expression, seemed dead. His neck was tightly enclosed by a dingy black silk cravat. The shadows concealed so well the part of the body that extended down-wards from the brown line drawn by this tattered neckpiece that a man of imagination might have taken his old head to be a silhouette created by chance, or an unframed Rembrandt portrait. The rim of the hat covering the old man's brow cast a black furrow across his upper face. This strange, albeit natural effect contrasted dramatically with the white wrinkles, the cold meanderings, and the sense of being washed out evident in this cadaverous physiognomy. Finally, the absence of any movement in the body, or any warmth in the gaze, was in keeping with a certain expression of gloomy dementia, with all the degrading symptoms that characterise idiocy, and made of this figure something vaguely funereal, something that no human words could describe. But an observer, and in particular a solicitor, would have also found in this stricken man the signs of a deep sorrow, the marks of a misery that had worn down that face, just as the drops of water falling from the sky on a beautiful marble sculpture eventually erode it. A doctor, an author, a magistrate would have guessed at an entire drama on seeing this sublime horror whose least merit was that it resembled those fantasies that painters enjoy doodling at the bottom of their lithographic stones[5] while chatting to their friends.

When he saw the solicitor, the stranger gave a start, and shuddered convulsively like poets when an unexpected noise distracts them from a fertile reverie in the midst of night and silence. The old man promptly took off his hat and stood up to greet the young man; the leather lining of his hat was doubtless thick with grease, for his wig remained stuck to it without his noticing, and revealed his bald skull horribly mutilated by a transversal scar that began at the crown of his head and expired over his right eye, forming a long, thick, prominent seam. The sudden removal of this dirty wig, which the poor man wore to conceal his wound, did not make either of the two men of law feel like laughing, as this split skull was such a terrible sight. The first thought suggested by the appearance of this wound was: 'His intelligence has leaked away through it!'

'If he's not Colonel Chabert, he must be a proud old trooper!' thought Boucard.

'Monsieur,' Derville said to him, 'to whom do I have the honour of speaking?'

'Colonel Chabert.'

'Which one?'

'The one who died at Eylau,' replied the old man.

Hearing this strange phrase, the clerk and the solicitor exchanged a glance that signified: 'He's mad!'

'Monsieur,' the Colonel resumed, 'it is to you alone that I would like to confide the secret of my situation.'

Something worthy of remark is the intrepidity natural to solicitors. Either because of their habit of receiving a great number of people, or because of the profound sense of the protection that the law affords them, or because of their confidence in their own ministry, they can go anywhere without fearing a thing, just like priests and doctors. Derville made a sign to Boucard, who disappeared.

'Monsieur,' the solicitor resumed, 'by day I am not too miserly with my time, but in the middle of the night, my minutes are precious. So be brief and concise. Get to the facts and don't digress. I myself will ask you when I need any explanations. Go on.'

After motioning his strange client to take a seat, the young man himself sat down at the table; but even as he lent his attention to the speech of the late Colonel, he leafed through his files.

'Monsieur,' the dead man said, 'you may know that I commanded a cavalry regiment at Eylau. I played an important part in the success of the celebrated charge led by Murat, which decided the battle in our favour. Unfortunately for me, my death is a historical fact registered in *Victories and Conquests*[6], where it is related in detail. We cut the three Russian lines in half, but when they immediately re-formed, we were obliged to return back through them in the opposite direction. As we were coming up towards the Emperor, after scattering the Russians, I met with a mass of enemy cavalry. I flung myself at the stubborn blighters. Two Russian officers, real giants both of them, attacked me simultaneously. One of them dealt me a sabre blow to the head which cut right through to a black silk cap I was wearing, and made a deep gash in my skull. I fell off my horse. Murat came to my aid, but rode right over my body, he and his entire company, fifteen hundred men, no less! My death was announced to the Emperor who took the trouble (he rather liked me, did the boss!) to find out if there really was no chance of saving the man to whom he owed such a dashing charge. He sent two surgeons with instructions to try and recognise me and bring me back to the ambulance wagons, telling them, perhaps rather negligently – he did have a lot on his hands at the time – "Just go and see if by any chance my poor Chabert is still alive." Those bloody medics who'd just seen me trampled underfoot by two regiments'-worth of horses no doubt couldn't be bothered to feel my pulse, and reported that I was indeed dead. So my death certificate was probably drawn up in accordance with the rules established by military jurisprudence.'

Hearing his client expressing himself with perfect lucidity and recounting such likely, albeit unusual, events, the young solicitor dropped his files, placed his left elbow on the table, rested his head in his hands and gazed fixedly at the Colonel.

'Do you know, Monsieur,' he broke in, 'that I am the solicitor of Countess Ferraud, the widow of Colonel Chabert?'

'My wife! Yes, Monsieur. – And so, after a hundred fruitless attempts with legal figures who all took me for a madman, I resolved to come and find you. I will tell you of my misfortunes later. First let me set out the facts, or explain to you how they must have happened rather than how they actually did happen. For certain circumstances, which only the Eternal Father can know, oblige me to present several of them as mere hypotheses. So, Monsieur, the wounds I received will probably have produced a tetanus, or put me in a critical state analogous to that of an illness called, I believe, catalepsy. How else can one explain the fact that I was, in accordance with the customs of war, stripped of my clothes, and thrown into the soldiers' common grave by the people responsible for the task of burying the dead? At this point, allow me to insert a detail that I was able only to find out after the event that one has to call my death. In 1814, I met in Stuttgart a former sergeant from my regiment. This dear friend, the only one willing to recognise me, and of whom I will tell you more shortly, explained the phenomenon of my preservation, telling me that my horse had been hit on the side by a cannon-ball at the same time that I myself was wounded. So the horse and its rider had both collapsed like a house of cards. Falling back either to the right or the left, I had no doubt been covered by the body of my horse, which saved me from being crushed by the horses or struck by cannon-balls. When I recovered consciousness, Monsieur, I was in a position and surrounded by an atmosphere that I could not convey to you even if I took all night. The little air I had to breathe was quite foul. I wanted to move, but there was no space. When I opened my eyes, I couldn't see a thing. The lack of air posed the biggest threat, and the one which made me realise my position most clearly. I realised that, where I was, no fresh air ever penetrated, and I was going to die. This thought assuaged the feeling of indescribable pain by which I had been awoken. My ears were filled with a loud ringing. I heard, or imagined I heard – I can't say for sure – groans uttered by the populace of corpses amongst whom I was lying. Although the memory of these movements is very unclear, and although my memories are quite confused, in spite of the even more profound impressions of suffering that I must have been feeling and that muddled my thoughts, there are nights on which I think I can still hear those stifled sighs! But there was something more horrible than the cries – a silence that I have never encountered anywhere else, the real silence of the grave. Eventually, raising my hands and feeling my way over the dead bodies, I realised there was a space between my head and the human manure lying over me. So I was able to probe the space that had been left me by a chance whose cause was unknown to me. It appears that, thanks to the carelessness or haste with which we had been piled pell-mell on top of one another, two bodies had fallen crosswise over me so as to form an angle like that of two cards leant against one another by a child laying the foundation of a castle. Ferreting around rapidly, as I couldn't hang about, I was lucky enough to find an arm that had got separated from its body – the arm of a Hercules! A nice bone to which I owed my life. Without this unexpected aid, I would have perished! But, with a fury you can easily imagine, I started to work my way through the bodies that lay between me and the layer of earth that had doubtless been thrown over us: I say us, as if there had been other men still alive there! I went about it with a will, Monsieur – that's why I'm here! But at present I don't know how I managed to break through the blanket of flesh that had formed a barrier between myself and life. You'd have thought I had three arms! This lever, that I used with some skill, continued to make it possible for me to get to the air between the bodies as I shifted them, and I breathed as little as possible. Finally I saw daylight, but through the snow, Monsieur! At that moment, I realised that I had a deep head-wound. Fortunately, my blood, or that from my comrades or from the skin-wounds of my horse, had, in coagulating, as it were applied a natural plaster to it. Despite that crust, I fainted when my skull came into contact with the snow. Nonetheless, the little heat remaining in my body melted the snow around me, and I found myself, when I recovered consciousness, in the middle of a little opening through which I shouted for as long as I could. But the sun was just rising at the time, and so there was very little chance I'd be heard. Were there already people in the fields? I lifted myself up, using my feet as supports to push against the dead men who were solidly built. You'll realise that it wasn't the right time to say to them: "A bit of respect for a courageous man in misfortune!" In short, Monsieur, after having experienced the pain – if such words can express my rage – of seeing over and over again those bloody Germans scarpering when they heard a voice that didn't seem to be coming from any man, I was finally pulled out by a woman who was bold enough or curious enough to come and take a look at my head, which seemed to have sprung up from the earth like a mushroom. This woman went to fetch her husband, and the two of them carried me to their poor hovel. It appears that I relapsed into catalepsy – permit me to use this expression to depict a state of which I have no idea, but which I have concluded, from what my hosts told me, must have been an effect of that illness. I remained for six months suspended between life and death, not speaking, or, when I did speak, talking nonsense. Finally my hosts had me taken into the hospital of Heilsberg. You will understand, Monsieur, that I had emerged from the belly of the common grave as naked as the day I emerged from my mother's womb; the result was that, six months later, when I remembered one fine morning that I had once been Colonel Chabert, and, recovering my reason, wanted to obtain from the people looking after me more respect than they were used to giving a poor devil, all my fellows in the same ward started laughing. Luckily for me, the surgeon had – out of a sense of his own importance – vouched for my recovery, and took a natural interest in his patient. When I spoke to him in a reasonably coherent way about my previous existence, that fine man (his name was Sparchmann) had a statement drawn up, in the juridical forms demanded by the laws of that country, concerning my miraculous escape from the common grave, and the time and day on which I had been found by my benefactress and her husband; the nature and exact position of my wounds, and, to complete these various details, a description of my appearance. Well, Monsieur – I have neither these important documents, nor the declaration that I made to a Heilsberg notary, to establish my identity! Ever since the day I was forced to leave that town by the fortunes of war, I have been wandering constantly like a vagabond, begging my bread, treated as a madman every time I recounted my adventure, and never having found, or earned, a single sou to procure the documents that could prove my words to be true, and restore me to social life. Often, my sufferings would keep me for months on end in little towns where every care was lavished on the sick Frenchman, but where they laughed in his face the minute he claimed to be Colonel Chabert. For a long time that laughter, and those doubts, drove me to acts of fury which did me no good and even led to me being locked up as a madman in Stuttgart. Indeed, you can easily judge whether or not, after a story like mine, there were sufficient reasons to have a man put away! After the two years of imprisonment I was forced to endure, after hearing my guards saying a thousand times over, "That's a poor man who thinks he's

Colonel Chabert!" to people who replied, "The poor man!", I became convinced of the impossibility of my own adventure, I became sad, resigned, tranquil, and gave up calling myself Colonel Chabert, so as to be able to leave prison and see France again. Oh, Monsieur! To see Paris again! It was a joy that I didn't…'

Colonel Chabert left his sentence unfinished and fell into a deep reverie that Derville refrained from interrupting.

'Monsieur, one fine day,' his client continued, 'one spring day, I was given my freedom and ten thalers, on the pretext that I was able to talk perfectly sensibly about all sorts of things and no longer called myself Colonel Chabert. Good Lord, at that period, and even now, at times, my name is disagreeable to me. I would like to be someone else. Whenever I think of my rights, it does for me. If my illness had rid me of all memory of my previous life, I would have been happy! I would have gone back into the army under some name or other, and who knows? I would have perhaps become a field marshal in Austria or Russia.'

'Monsieur,' said the solicitor, 'you're confusing me. I feel I'm dreaming as I listen to you. Please, let's leave it there for a while.'

'You are,' the Colonel said, with a melancholy expression, 'the only person who has listened to me so patiently. No man of law has ever been prepared to loan me ten napoleons so as to have sent over from Germany the papers necessary for me to go to Court…'

'Go to Court?' said the solicitor, forgetting the painful situation his client was in now as he listened to the story of his former miseries.

'But Monsieur, isn't Countess Ferraud my wife? She has an income of three thousand livres that belongs to me, and refuses to give me two sous. When I tell all this to the solicitors, to men of good sense; when I, a beggar, suggest bringing a lawsuit against a count and a countess; when I, a dead man, rise in rebellion against a death certificate, a marriage certificate and birth certificates, they show me to the door, depending on their character, either with that frigidly polite air assumed by people when trying to get rid of an unhappy man, or else brutally, like people who think they're dealing with a schemer or a madman. I was buried under the dead, now I am buried under the living, under the whole of society, which is trying to push me back down into the earth!'

'Monsieur, please do go on,' said the solicitor.

'*Please*,' exclaimed the unhappy old man as he seized the young man's hand, 'that's the first polite word I have heard since…'

The Colonel burst into tears. His voice was choked by gratitude. The penetrating and inexpressible eloquence that lies in a man's gaze, his gestures, his very silence, all finally convinced Derville and touched him deeply.

'Listen, Monsieur,' he told his client, 'this evening I won three hundred francs at the gambling table; I can easily put half that sum towards making another man happy. I will begin the legal proceedings necessary to procure the documents you have told me about, and until they arrive I'll give you an allowance of a hundred sous per day. If you really are Colonel Chabert, you'll easily forgive the modesty of the loan that a young man who still has to make his fortune can make you. Carry on.'

The self-styled Colonel stood for a moment rooted to the spot, dumbstruck: the extremity of his misfortune had doubtless destroyed all his hopes. If he was out to get back his military dignity, his wealth, his own identity, perhaps it was because he was driven by that inexplicable feeling that is latent in the hearts of all men, and to which we owe the endeavours of alchemists: the craving for glory, the discoveries of astronomy and physics – all that impels man to grow in stature by multiplying himself through deeds or ideas. The Colonel's ego was, to his own mind, merely a secondary consideration, just as the vanity of winning or the pleasure of gain become dearer to the gambler than the object of his wager. So the young solicitor's words appeared like a miracle to this man who for ten years had been rejected by his wife, by justice, by the entire social fabric. To find a solicitor offering him those ten gold pieces that had been refused him for so long by so many people and in so many different ways! The Colonel resembled that lady who, having suffered a fever for fifteen years, thought on the day she was cured that she had merely exchanged one illness for another. There are types of happiness you have lost any hope of enjoying; the happiness arrives like a thunderbolt, and consumes you. Thus it was that the poor man's gratitude was too intense for him to express it. He would have appeared frigid to superficial observers, but Derville could guess at the great probity behind this man's stupor. A pretender would have had more of a gift of the gab.

'Where had I got to?' said the Colonel, with the naivety of a child or a soldier, for there is often something childish in a true soldier, and almost always something soldierly in a child – especially in France.

'Stuttgart. You'd just got out of prison,' replied the solicitor.

'Do you know my wife?' asked the Colonel.

'Yes,' replied Derville, with a nod.

'How does she look?'

'As beautiful as ever.'

The old man gestured with his hand, and seemed to be mulling over some secret sorrow with that grave and solemn resignation that characterises men who have gone through the blood and fire of battlefields.

'Monsieur,' he said, with a kind of gaiety; for this poor Colonel could after all breathe again, he had emerged a second time from the tomb, he had just melted a layer of snow more difficult to dissolve than the one which had long ago frozen over his head, and he breathed deeply as if he had just escaped from a dungeon. 'Monsieur,' he said, 'if I'd been a handsome fellow, none of my misfortunes would have happened. Women believe men when they stuff the word "love" into every phrase they utter. *Then* they come running, they dash here and there, they go out of their way for you, they plot, they corroborate your version of events, they do their damned best for the man they like. How could I have ever persuaded a woman to take my side? I had a face as gloomy as a requiem mass, I was dressed like a tattered revolutionary, I looked more like an Eskimo than a Frenchman – and yet I was the most dapper dandy around, back in 1799! I was Chabert, a count of the Empire! Well anyway, the very same day that I was thrown out onto the streets like a dog, who should I meet but the sergeant I've already told you about. He was called Boutin, this friend of mine. The poor devil and I were the most broken-down jades I'd ever seen in my life; I spotted him out for a stroll, and though I recognised *him*, it was quite impossible for him to guess who *I* was. We went into a tavern together. There, when I told him my name, Boutin's mouth split open into peals of laughter like a mortar going off. His merriment, Monsieur, wounded me as deeply as anything I ever felt! It showed me, without beating about the bush, all the ways I had changed! So I was unrecognisable, even to the eye of the humblest and most grateful of my friends! In bygone days I'd saved Boutin's life, that was a favour I'd long owed him. I won't tell you how he did me this good turn. It happened in Italy, in Ravenna. The house where Boutin stopped me being stabbed to death wasn't a particularly savoury place. At that time I wasn't a colonel, just an ordinary cavalryman, like Boutin. Happily there were details in the story that nobody else apart from us could possibly have known; and when I reminded him of them, his incredulity faded. Then I related to him the incidents of my strange existence. Although my eyes and my voice had been, so he told me, quite transformed by misfortune, and although I had lost all my hair, my teeth and my eyebrows, and was now as white as an albino, he finally recognised his colonel in the shape of a beggar, after sounding me out with a thousand questions to which I victoriously gave the right answer. He told me the story of *his* adventures, which were every bit as extraordinary as mine: he had just returned from the borders of China, where he had headed after escaping from Siberia. He told me of the disasters of the Russian campaign and Napoleon's first abdication. This piece of news was one of the things that hurt me most! We were two odd bits of debris who had rolled across the globe in the same way pebbles roll through the ocean waves, swept from one shore to another by the storms. Between us we had seen Egypt, Syria, Spain, Russia, Holland, Germany, Italy, Dalmatia, England, China, Tartary, and Siberia; all we needed now was to spend some time in India and America! In the end, being more sprightly than me, Boutin agreed to take himself off to Paris with all the speed he could muster so as to inform my wife of the state I was in. I wrote a letter to Madame Chabert, giving her all the details. This was the fourth letter, Monsieur! If I'd had any relatives, none of this, perhaps, would have happened, but, I have to confess, I'm a foundling, a soldier whose inheritance was his courage, whose family was the whole world, whose fatherland was France, whose only protector was the good Lord. No, I'm wrong – I did have a father: the Emperor! Ah, if I could only see him still standing there, that fine fellow! If only he could see *his Chabert*, as he called me, in the state I'm in, he'd fly into a rage. Well, what can we expect… Our sun has set, and now we all feel the cold. After all, it could be political events that explained my wife's silence! Boutin set off. *He* was all right! He had two well-trained polar bears to help him earn a living. I couldn't go with him; the pain I was in didn't allow me to make long journeys. I wept, Monsieur, when we separated, after we had walked for as long as my state permitted, me, his bears, and him. At Karlsruhe I had an attack of neuralgia in the head, and spent six weeks lying on the straw in an inn! I'd never be done, Monsieur, if I had to relate all the miseries of my life as a beggar. But moral suffering, besides which physical pain fades in comparison, arouses less pity, because you can't see it. I remember weeping outside a hotel in Strasbourg where once upon a time I'd thrown a party, and where they wouldn't give me a thing, not even a scrap of bread. Having agreed beforehand with Boutin on the route I was to take, I'd go along to every post office to ask if there was a letter or any money for me. I reached Paris without receiving anything. How much despair I had to swallow! – Boutin must be dead, I told myself. And it was true, the poor devil had met his end at Waterloo. I learnt of his death later on, by chance. His mission to my wife had doubtless met with no success. Finally I entered Paris at the same time as the Cossacks. For me it was one cause of grief on top of another. Seeing the Russians in France, I quite forgot that I had neither shoes on my feet nor money in my pocket.

Yes, Monsieur, my clothes were in tatters. The night before my arrival I was forced to bivouac in the woods at Claye. The night chill probably set off another attack of some illness or other as I was crossing the *Faubourg* Saint-Martin. I collapsed, practically unconscious, outside the door of an ironmonger. When I woke up, I was in a bed at the Hôtel-Dieu[7]. There I stayed for a month, feeling relatively well. I was soon turned out. I was penniless, but I was in good health and able to set my feet on the streets of my beloved Paris. With what joy and haste I made my way to the rue du Mont-Blanc, where I thought my wife must be living in one of my town houses. Damn! The rue du Mont-Blanc had changed into the rue de la Chaussée-d'Antin. My house was no longer there – it had been sold off and torn down. Speculators had built several new houses in my gardens. Unaware that my wife had married Monsieur Ferraud, I could obtain no information. Finally I went to see an old solicitor who had previously looked after my business. The fellow had died after transferring his clientele to a younger man. The latter told me, to my great astonishment, that my will had been opened and my estate settled, and that my wife had married again and now had two children. When I told him I was Colonel Chabert, he started to laugh so uproariously that I left him without making the least remark. My detention in Stuttgart made me wary of ending up in Charenton[8], and I resolved to act with caution. Anyway, Monsieur, now that I knew where my wife lived, I made my way to her house, my heart filled with hope. Well,' said the Colonel, with a gesture of intense but restrained rage, 'I was not received when I had myself announced under a borrowed name, and the day when I assumed my real name, I was turned away from her door. So as to see the Countess returning from the ball or a show in the early hours, I spent entire nights posted at the bollard of her carriage entrance. I would peer into her carriage as it dashed past me as quick as lightning, and in which I could barely make out the shape of that woman who is my wife and who no longer belongs to me! Ah! Ever since that day I have lived for vengeance!' exclaimed the old man hoarsely, suddenly stretching to his full length in front of Derville. 'She knows that I exist; since my return, she has received two letters from me, written in my own hand. She doesn't love me any more! And I don't even know whether I love her or hate her! I want her and curse her by turns. She owes her wealth and her happiness to me; well, she hasn't even given me the slightest bit of help! There are times when I don't know what will become of me!'

With these words, the old soldier sat back heavily on his chair, and resumed his former immobility. Derville remained silent, intently gazing at his client.

'It's a serious business,' he finally said, mechanically. 'Even if we admit the authenticity of the documents that must be in Heilsberg, nothing proves to me that we can win the case at once. The trial will go before three courts in succession. We have to think about a case like this with a calm head: it's altogether exceptional.'

'Oh,' the Colonel replied coldly, raising his head with a gesture of pride, 'if I'm defeated, I'll be happy to die; but I won't go alone.'

And then, all at once, the old man had vanished. The eyes of a man full of energy shone with the rekindled flames of desire and revenge.

'We might have to compromise,' said the solicitor.

'Compromise?' repeated Colonel Chabert. 'Am I alive or am I dead?'

'Monsieur,' continued the solicitor, 'you will, I hope, follow my advice. Your case will be my case. You will soon realise how much interest I take in your situation, which is almost unexampled in all the pomp and circumstance of legal annals. Meanwhile, I'll let you have a letter for my notary, and on your signature he'll give you fifty francs every ten days. It wouldn't be appropriate for you to be seen coming to me for help. If you *are* Colonel Chabert, you mustn't be at the mercy of anyone. I'll treat this money paid in advance as a loan. You have property to recover; you're a wealthy man.'

The delicacy of this last remark drew tears from the old chap. Derville stood up abruptly, for it was not perhaps quite the right thing for a solicitor to show any emotion; he went over into his study, and returned with an unsealed letter which he handed to Colonel Chabert. When the poor man held it in his hands, he could feel two gold coins through the paper.

'Would you like to tell me which documents are involved, and the name of the town and the kingdom?' asked the solicitor.

The Colonel dictated the information, and checked the spelling of the place names; then he took his hat in one hand, gazed at Derville, held out his other hand – a calloused hand – to him, and said quite simply: 'My word, Monsieur, after the Emperor, you are the man to whom I will have owed most! You are a hero.'

The solicitor heartily shook the Colonel's hand, led him out to the stairwell, and gave him light.

'Boucard,' said Derville to his chief clerk, 'I've just heard a story that will perhaps cost me twenty-five louis. If it turns out I've been fleeced, I won't regret wasting my money – I'll have seen the most skilful actor of our generation.'

When the Colonel found himself back out in the street and standing next to a lamp-post, he took from the letter the two twenty-franc coins that the solicitor had given him, and looked at them for a while by the lamplight. This was the first time in nine years that he had seen gold.

'I'm going to be able to smoke cigars!' he said to himself.

Some three months after Colonel Chabert's nocturnal consultation at Derville's, the notary entrusted with disbursing the half-pay the solicitor gave to his singular client came to see him to confer on a serious matter, and began by asking him to return six hundred francs given to the ex-soldier.

'So your latest pastime is maintaining the old army?' said this notary, whose name was Crottat, with a laugh. He was a young man who had just bought the law firm where he was chief clerk, and whose boss had just fled after going catastrophically bankrupt.

'Thank you, Master Crottat, for reminding me of that business,' replied Derville. 'My philanthropy won't go beyond twenty-five louis; I fear I have already let my patriotism get the better of me.'

At the very moment Derville uttered these last words, he caught sight of the parcels his chief clerk had left on his desk. His eyes were struck by the sight of the oblong, square, triangular, red, and blue stamps stuck on one particular letter by the postal services of Prussia, Austria, Bavaria, and France.

'Ah!' he said with a laugh, 'here's the final act of the play, let's see if I've been caught out.' He took up the letter and opened it, but was unable to read it as it was in German. – 'Boucard, go and get this letter translated, and come back straight away,' said Derville, opening his office door and holding the letter out to his chief clerk.

The Berlin notary to whom the solicitor had written informed him in this letter that the documents Derville had asked to be sent would reach him a few days after this notice. The papers were in perfectly good order, he said, and accompanied by all the ratifications necessary to be valid in law. Furthermore, he begged to inform him that almost all the witnesses of the facts noted in the reports were still living in Preussisch-Eylau; and the woman to whom Count Chabert owed his life was still in one of the suburbs of Heilsberg.

'This is getting serious,' exclaimed Derville, when Boucard had finally explained the substance of the letter to him.

'Well then, young fellow,' he continued, turning to the notary, 'I'm going to need some information that must be available in your office. Wasn't it at that old rascal Roguin's that –'

'We call him "the unfortunate and unhappy Roguin",' said Monsieur Alexandre Crottat with a laugh, interrupting Derville.

'Wasn't it at that unfortunate man's, the one who's just run off with eight hundred thousand francs from his clients and reduced several families to despair, that they settled the succession of Colonel Chabert? I seem to remember reading as much in our Ferraud documents.'

'Yes,' Crottat replied, 'I was third clerk at the time, I copied that settlement out and studied it closely. Rose Chapotel, wife and widow of Hyacinthe Chabert, Count of the Empire, Grand Officer of the Legion of Honour; they'd got married without a contract, so they owned their goods in common. As far as I remember, their assets amounted to six hundred thousand francs. Before his marriage, Count Chabert had drawn up a will in favour of the Paris hospices, making over to them a quarter of whatever wealth he owned at the time of his death, and the public domain would inherit the other quarter. There was an auction, with a sale and division of the property, as the solicitors soon got cracking. At the time of the settlement, the monster who was then governing France[9] issued an ordinance granting to the Colonel's widow the portion owed to the inland revenue.'

'So Count Chabert's personal wealth amounts to only three hundred thousand francs.'

'Quite so, old chap!' replied Crottat. 'You sometimes hit the nail on the head, you solicitors, though sometimes you're accused of twisting things when you argue for and against equally well.'

Count Chabert, whose address was written at the bottom of the first receipt delivered by the notary to Derville, was living in the *Faubourg* Saint-Marceau, in the rue du Petit-Banquier, with an old sergeant of the Imperial Guard who had since become a dairyman, called Vergniaud. When he arrived there, Derville was forced to continue his quest for his client on foot, for his coachman refused to risk entering an unpaved street whose ruts were a little too deep for the wheels of a cabriolet. Looking round on every side, the solicitor finally found, in the part of the street next to the boulevard, between two walls built out of a mixture of bones and earth, two crumbling pillars made of rubble, which passing vehicles had knocked and dented, despite two pieces of wood set there as posts. These pillars supported a beam of wood covered with a coping of tiles, on which were written in red these words: VERGNIAUD, DAREYMAN. To the right of this name could be seen some eggs, and to the left a cow, all painted in white. The gate was open, and no doubt remained open all day long. At the far end of a quite spacious courtyard there rose, opposite the gate, a house – if indeed the name of house fits one of those hovels built in the Paris suburbs, resembling nothing on earth, not even the most pathetic dwellings of the countryside, whose poverty they share without having anything of their poetry. After all, out in the fields, such huts have a certain grace, produced by the purity of the air, the green grass, the sight of the fields, a hill, a winding path, vines, a flowering hedge, the moss of the thatched roofs, and the various rustic implements; but in Paris the poverty merely seems all the greater because of its ugliness. Although of recent construction, this house seemed on the verge of collapse. None of the materials used in its building had been put to their proper use; they all came from the demolitions which are a daily occurrence in Paris. Derville read on a shutter made with the planks from a shop sign the words: *Novelty gift shop*. The windows bore no resemblance to one another and were placed at bizarre angles. The ground floor, which seemed the habitable part, was raised on one side, while on the other side the rooms were completely overshadowed by a small hillock. Between the gate and the house stretched a pond filled with manure, into which drained the rainwater and water from the washing. The wall against which this ramshackle abode was propped, a wall which seemed a bit more secure than the others, was decorated with hutches where real rabbits produced their numerous families. To the right of the carriage-door rose the cowshed topped by a hayloft, linked to the house by a dairy. To the right was a farmyard, a stable, and a pigsty which had been topped off, like the roof of the house, by rotten planks of wood nailed together and clumsily covered with rush. Like almost all the places where the ingredients for the copious meal that Paris devours every day are cooked, the courtyard into which Derville stepped showed traces of the urgent haste required by the necessity of reaching your destination punctually every day. Those great dented tin churns in which milk is transported, and the pots containing the cream, had been strewn around pell-mell outside the dairy, together with their linen stoppers. The torn and tattered rags used to wipe them were floating in the sunlight stretched out on lengths of string attached to stakes. The pacific horse, a member of that race employed only in the dairy industry, had taken a few steps forward from his cart and was standing outside the stable, whose door was shut. A goat was grazing on the leaves of the spindly, dusty vine that adorned the yellow, cracked wall of the house. A cat was squatting on the cream pots, licking them out. The hens took fright at Derville's approach, and squawked and scampered away, and the guard-dog started barking.

'To think the man who ensured the victorious outcome of the Battle of Eylau is living here!' said Derville to himself, taking in at a single glance the whole sorry spectacle.

The house had been left under the protection of three kids. One of them had climbed on the ridge-piece of a cart loaded with unripe hay, and was chucking stones into the chimney of the house next door, in the hope they would fall into the cooking pot. The second was trying to drag a pig over onto the plank floor of the cart that had been lowered to the ground, while the third, hanging onto the other end, was waiting for the pig to be in place before hoisting it aloft by tipping up the cart. When Derville asked them if this was the place where Monsieur Chabert lived, none of them replied, and all three stared at him with supercilious stupidity, if it is permissible to use these two words together. Derville reiterated his questions without success. Irritated by the mocking expression of these three little rascals, he came out with a few of those facetious insults which young men feel entitled to address to children, and the boys broke their silence with a brutal laugh. Derville grew angry. The Colonel heard him and emerged from a low little room situated near the dairy, appearing on the threshold with a military composure that words cannot describe. In his mouth was clamped one of those remarkably *seasoned* pipes (in the technical term used by smokers), one of those humble clay pipes called cutties. He lifted the rim of a horribly filthy cap, spotted Derville and, taking the shortest route to reach his benefactor, walked across the heap of manure, shouting a friendly, 'Silence in the ranks!' to the boys. They immediately fell respectfully silent, showing how much influence the old soldier had over them.

'Why didn't you write to me?' he said to Derville. 'Go along by the cowshed! Look, just there, the path is paved,' he exclaimed, seeing the solicitor hesitating, as he didn't want to get his feet wet in the manure.

Hopping carefully from one spot to the next, Derville reached the threshold of the door from which the Colonel had emerged. Chabert appeared somewhat aggrieved at having to receive him in the room he occupied. And indeed, Derville could see only a single chair there. The Colonel's bed consisted of a few bundles of straw over which his hostess had stretched two or three bits and pieces of old tapestry, picked up heaven knows where, and used by milkmaids to cover the seats of their carts. The room had a simple mud floor. Its walls, treated with saltpetre, green with mould and full of cracks, gave off such a musty dampness that the wall against which the Colonel slept was lined with a rush mat. The well-known greatcoat was hanging from a nail. Two grimy pairs of boots were lying in a corner. There was no sight of any clean linen. On the worm-eaten table, the *Bulletins of the Grand Army*[10] reissued by Plancher lay open, and seemed to constitute the Colonel's reading matter. His face was calm and serene amidst this poverty. His visit to Derville seemed to have altered the cast of his features, on which the solicitor detected traces of a more mellow frame of mind, a particular gleam imparted to his face by hope.

'Does the smoke from my pipe bother you?' he said, holding out to the solicitor the chair, which had only half its straw seating left.

'But Colonel, this is a dreadful place for you to be in.'

Derville uttered these words with the involuntary mistrust that comes naturally to solicitors, a product of the deplorable experience they gain early on from the terrible and mysterious dramas of which they are witness.

'Here,' he said to himself, 'we see a man who has certainly used my money to satisfy the trooper's three theological virtues: gambling, wine, and women!'

'You're right, Monsieur, we're not exactly living in the lap of luxury. It's a bivouac, made easier to share because of friendship, but…' Here the soldier darted a piercing glance at the lawyer. 'But I've done no wrong to anyone, I've never turned anyone away, and I sleep with a good conscience.'

The solicitor reflected that it would not be tactful to ask his client to account for the sums of money he had loaned him, and he contented himself with saying, 'So why didn't you want to come to a more central part of Paris where you could have lived just as cheaply as here, but more comfortably?'

'But the fine people I am living with,' replied the Colonel, 'had taken me in and fed me gratis for a whole year! How could I leave them the minute I had a bit of money? And then, the father of those three lads is an old *Egyptian*.'

'What do you mean – an Egyptian?'

'That's what we call the troopers who came back from the expedition to Egypt, in which I took part. Not only are all those who returned like brothers, but Vergniaud was in my regiment at the time, we shared our water in the desert. Anyway, I still haven't finished teaching his nippers to read.'

'He could have given you somewhere nicer to live in return for the money you pay him, couldn't he?'

'Bah!' said the Colonel, 'his children sleep on straw just like me! He and his wife don't have anywhere better to sleep, they're really poor – you see? They've taken on a business beyond their means. But if I ever get my fortune back!... Anyway, that's enough of that.'

'Colonel, I expect to receive, tomorrow or the day after, your papers from Heilsberg. The woman who freed you is still alive!'

'Bloody money! To think I don't have any!' he cried, flinging his pipe to the ground.

A *seasoned* pipe is a precious pipe for a smoker; but the movement with which he threw it down came to him so naturally, and from such a generous impulse, that all smokers – and even the customs and excise department – would have forgiven him for this act of treason against tobacco. The angels would perhaps have picked up the pieces.

'Colonel, your case is extremely complicated,' Derville said to him, stepping out of the room so he could stroll up and down outside the house in the sunshine.

'It seems perfectly simple to me,' said the soldier. 'They thought I was dead, and here I am! Give me back my wife and my wealth; give me the rank of general, as I deserve, for I was made a colonel in the Imperial Guard on the eve of the Battle of Eylau.'

'That's not how things work in the legal world,' replied Derville. 'Listen. You are Count Chabert, I'm happy to accept as much, but you have to prove it in a court of law to people who have every interest in denying your existence. So your papers will be contested. This in turn will lead to a dozen or so preliminary questions. They will all go, after full argument, to the High Court, and will require expensive lawsuits that will get dragged out, however energetically I try to push them along. Your opponents will demand an enquiry which we won't be able to refuse, and which will perhaps necessitate a rogatory commission in Prussia. But let's suppose everything goes as well as it can: let's imagine that your identity as Colonel Chabert is speedily recognised in law. Do we know how the question raised by the perfectly innocent bigamy of Countess Ferraud will be adjudged? In your case, the point of law at issue lies outside the Civil Code, and judges can decide it only in accordance with the laws of conscience, as the jury does in those delicate questions raised by the strange social phenomena met with in certain criminal trials. But you had no children from your marriage, whereas Count Ferraud has two from his, and the judges can declare null and void the marriage where the ties are weakest, in favour of the marriage where the ties are strongest, once it is accepted that those contracting it acted in good faith. Do you think you'll be able to take the moral high ground if you insist on sticking to your guns and holding onto a wife who doesn't love you any more – you at your age and in the circumstances you find yourself in? You will be up against your wife and her husband, two powerful people who will be able to influence the courts. So the lawsuit seems set to last for ever. You'll find your old age is one long tale of woe.'

'What about my wealth?'

'Do you really think you're all that wealthy?'

'Didn't I have an income of thirty thousand livres?'

'My dear Colonel, in 1799, before your marriage, you made a will bequeathing a quarter of your wealth to the hospices.'

'That's true.'

'Well, once you were deemed to be dead, wasn't it necessary to proceed to draw up an inventory and settle the estate so that quarter could indeed be given to the hospices? Your wife had no qualms about cheating the poor. The inventory, in which she doubtless refrained from mentioning the cash and the jewels, referred to only a fraction of the silverware, and made sure the moveables were valued at only two-thirds of their real price, either so as to benefit herself, or to avoid paying death duties, and also because the auctioneers are responsible for their valuations… The inventory drawn up amounted to assets of six hundred thousand francs. For her part, your widow had a right to half. Everything was put on sale, she bought it all up, making a profit on everything, and the hospices got their seventy-five thousand francs. Then, as some of your money belonged to the inland revenue, given the fact that you hadn't mentioned your wife in your will, the Emperor made over to your widow, by decree, the share that fell to the public domain. How much money do you have a right to now? Three hundred thousand francs, no more, minus costs.'

'And you call that justice?' said Colonel Chabert, dumbstruck.

'But of course…'

'Fine justice!'

'That's how it is, my poor Colonel. As you see, what you thought would be easy isn't at all so. Madame Ferraud might even decide to keep the share given her by the Emperor.'

'But she wasn't a widow, the decree is null and void…'

'Agreed. But you can argue it both ways. Listen. In these circumstances, I think that a deal would be the best way of bringing the case to an end, both for you and for her. You'll gain a more considerable fortune than any you have a right to.'

'It would mean selling my wife!'

'With an income of twenty-four thousand francs, you will have, in the position you find yourself in, plenty of women who will suit you better than your wife, and will make you happier. I'm planning to go and see Countess Ferraud today, as a matter of fact, to test the waters, but I didn't want to take this step without warning you beforehand.'

'Let's go and see her together…'

'With you in the state you're in?' said the solicitor. 'No, Colonel, no. You could lose your case at a stroke…'

'Is my case winnable?'

'On every count,' replied Derville. 'But, my dear Colonel Chabert, there's one thing you're ignoring. I'm not wealthy, my job isn't fully paid. If the courts grant you a partial payment, a sum of money as an advance on your fortune, they will do so only once they've recognised your titles as Count Chabert, Grand Officer of the Legion of Honour.'

'Hm, yes, I *am* a Grand Officer of the Legion, I was forgetting,' he said, naively.

'Well anyway,' continued Derville, 'until then don't you think you'll need someone to plead your case, as well as pay for solicitors, adjourn and settle judgements, get the bailiffs on your side, and live? The costs of the preparatory hearings will amount to more than twelve or fifteen thousand francs, at a guess. *I* don't have that much – I'm lumbered with the huge interest I have to pay to the man who lent me the money to buy my office. And where on earth will *you* find it?'

Big tears fell from the poor soldier's haggard eyes and rolled down his wrinkled cheeks. At the thought of all these difficulties he felt discouraged. The social and judicial world weighed on his breast like a nightmare.

'I'll go to the foot of the column on the Place Vendôme,' he exclaimed, 'and there I'll cry out: "I am Colonel Chabert, the one who broke through the great Russian square at Eylau!" At least the bronze statue[11] will recognise me!'

'And they'll probably cart you off to Charenton.'

At that dreaded name, the soldier's exaltation evaporated.

'Might I not have a chance of success with the war ministry?'

'Oh, those bureaucrats!' said Derville. 'Go ahead, but make sure you have a proper judicial decision declaring your death certificate null and void. Those officials would like to destroy everyone left from Empire days.'

The Colonel stood for a moment, dumbfounded, motionless, gazing unseeingly ahead, lost in an abyss of bottomless despair. Military justice is all cut and dried, it passes judgement in a rough and ready way, and almost always comes to the right decision; this justice was the only sort Chabert was acquainted with. When he saw the labyrinth of difficulties he would have to venture into, when he saw how much money he needed to embark on the journey, the poor soldier felt a mortal blow to that faculty particular to man called the *will*. It seemed impossible for him to live involved in litigation, it would have been a thousand times easier for him to stay a poor beggar, to sign up as a cavalryman if there was a regiment that would take him. His physical and moral sufferings had already severely affected his body and left their mark on some of his most important organs. He was verging on one of those illnesses for which medical science has no name, and whose seat is, as it were, variable, like the nervous system which appears the most vulnerable of all those in our internal machinery – a disease which we can only call the 'spleen' of unhappiness. However serious this invisible but real illness might be, it could still be cured by a successful outcome. To shake that vigorous organism, all that was needed was a new obstacle, an unexpected turn of events that would snap its weakened springs and produce those hesitations, those poorly understood, spasmodic acts that physiologists observe in people ruined by misfortune.

Recognising the symptoms of a deep depression overwhelming his client, Derville said, 'Take heart, the case is bound to turn out in your favour. But just think whether *you* can put all your trust in me, and blindly accept the result I will decide is the best one for you.'

'Do whatever you want,' said Chabert.

'Yes, but will you abandon yourself to me, like a man marching to his death?'

'Does it mean I'm going to remain bereft of identity and name? Is that tolerable?'

'That's not how I see it,' said the solicitor. 'We'll try and reach an amicable settlement annulling your death certificate and your marriage, so that you can receive what is due to you. Thanks to the influence of Count Ferraud, you'll even be put on the army list as a general, and you'll probably be given a pension.'

'Very well!' replied Chabert, 'I entrust myself entirely to you.'

'So I'll send you a power of attorney to sign,' said Derville. 'Goodbye: chin up! If you need money, you can count on me.'

Chabert shook Derville's hand warmly, and remained with his back to the wall, without the strength to do any more than watch him go. Like everyone who knows little about the law, he was frightened by the idea of this unexpected trial. During their conversation, the face of a man posted in the street to watch for Derville's exit had peered out from behind one of the pillars of the carriage entrance. When Derville came out, he accosted him. He was an old man dressed in a blue jacket, white pleated overalls of the type worn by brewers, and wearing a cap of otter skin on his head. His face was brown and furrowed with deep wrinkles, but his cheek-bones were reddened by toil and tanned by a life out of doors.

'Excuse me, Monsieur, for taking the liberty of speaking to you,' he said to Derville, seizing him by the arm, 'but when I saw you I suspected you might be the friend of our general.'

'So?' said Derville, 'what makes you interested in him? Who are you, anyway?' added the mistrustful solicitor.

'I'm Louis Vergniaud,' he answered straight away. 'And I'd like a word or two with you.'

'So you're the man who's put him in accommodation like *that*?'

'Sorry, Monsieur, really I am, but he has the finest room. I'd have given him mine, if I'd only had the one. I'd have slept in the stable. A man who's been through the things he has, who's teaching my nippers to read, a general, an Egyptian, the first lieutenant I ever served under... think I'd see him hard done by? At all events, he's got the best room. I've shared everything I have with him. Unfortunately it wasn't a lot – bread, milk, eggs; well, you have to take the rough with the smooth. I'm happy to do it. Only... he's offended us.'

'He has?'

'Yes, Monsieur, offended us, not to put too fine a point on it. I've taken on a business beyond our means, and he realised as much. It bothered him, and so he went and groomed my horse · for me! I said to him, I said: "Now, now, General!" – "Bah!" says he, "I don't want to be a slacker, and I'm an old hand at brushing down the horses." So I'd drawn up the bill to pay for my cowshed to a man named Orados... Do you know him, Monsieur?'

'My dear fellow, I don't have time to listen to you. Just tell me how the Colonel's offended you!'

'He *has* offended us and all, Monsieur, as sure as my name's Louis Vergniaud, and my wife's wept for it. He found out from the neighbours that we didn't have a penny to put towards our bill. Without breathing a word, the old fellow saved up everything you gave him, kept an eye open for the bill, and paid it off. The old slyboots! My wife and me, we knew as he had no tobacco, poor old chap, and he was having to do without! And now! Every morning there he is with his cigars! I'd rather sell myself, I would... No! anyway, we're offended. So I'd like to suggest you loan us, you as is such a decent fellow, so he's told us, a hundred écus or so on our business, so we can get some clothes made for him and decorate his room a bit. He thought he was paying us back, you know? Well, quite the opposite, the old chap has put us in his debt, you see... and it's offended us! He didn't ought to have snubbed us like that. He's really offended us! And we're friends! Word of honour as a gentleman, as sure as my name is Louis Vergniaud, I'd rather enlist than not give you that money back...'

Derville stared at the dairyman, and took a few steps back to take another look at the house, the yard, the piles of manure, the cowshed, the rabbits, and the children.

'Well, well, I do believe that one of the characteristics of virtue lies in not being a landowner,' he said to himself. 'Go on with you, you'll get your hundred écus – and more! But it won't be me that gives them to you; the Colonel will be rich enough to help you out, and I don't want to deprive him of that pleasure.'

'Will it be soon?'

'Oh yes.'

'Ah, thank God, my wife will be so pleased!'

And the dairyman's tanned face seemed to brighten up.

'Now then,' said Derville to himself, as he climbed back into his cabriolet, 'let's go and pay a visit to our enemy. Let's not show our hand, let's try and find out what cards *she* holds, and win the game at a single stroke. Should we frighten her? She's a woman. What are women most frightened of? Well, women are only frightened of...'

He started to turn over in his mind the Countess' situation, and fell into one of those meditations to which great politicians are prone when they dream up their plans and try to imagine the secrets of the opposing camp. Aren't solicitors to some extent men of state responsible for private affairs? A quick glance at the circumstances of Count Ferraud and his wife is necessary here to convey just how brilliant a solicitor Derville was.

Count Ferraud was the son of a former councillor in the Parliament of Paris, who had emigrated under the Terror, and who, though he saved his head, lost his fortune. He returned home under the Consulate and remained constantly faithful to the interests of Louis XVIII, in whose circles his father had moved before the Revolution. He thus belonged to that part of the *Faubourg* Saint-Germain that nobly resisted the seductions of Napoleon[12]. The reputation for capability acquired by the young count, then simply called Monsieur Ferraud, made him the object of the Emperor's flirtatious flattery: Napoleon was frequently just as proud of his conquests among the aristocracy as he was of winning a battle. He promised the Count he would restore his title and his unsold property, and dangled before him in the distance the prospect of a ministerial or senatorial post. The Emperor failed. Monsieur Ferraud was, at the time of the supposed death of Count Chabert, a young man of twenty-six, without a fortune, endowed with an agreeable appearance, blessed with success, and adopted by the *Faubourg* Saint-Germain as one of its leading lights; but Countess Chabert had been so adept in her handling of her husband's succession that after eighteen months of widowhood she possessed an income of some forty thousand livres. Her marriage with the young count was not seen as anything new by the coteries of the *Faubourg* Saint-Germain. Pleased with this marriage, which chimed in with his idea of fusing the old classes and the new, Napoleon restored to Madame Chabert the portion of the Colonel's succession that fell to the inland revenue; but Napoleon's hopes were again dashed. Madame Ferraud did not just love the young man as her lover, she had equally been seduced by the idea of gaining entry to that haughty society which, despite coming down in the world, still dominated the imperial Court. All her vanity was flattered by this marriage, just as much as was her passion. She was about to become a *society lady*. When the *Faubourg* Saint-Germain realised that the young Count's marriage had not been a defection, its salons were thrown open to his wife. Along came the Restoration. Count Ferraud's political fortune was a long time in coming. He well understood the exigency of the position in which Louis XVIII found himself, and he was one of the initiates who were waiting for the 'abyss opened by revolutions to be closed' – for this royal phrase, which so many liberals made fun of, concealed a political meaning. Nonetheless, the ordinance quoted in the long clerkly sentence that begins this story had restored to him two forests and a piece of land whose value had increased substantially during the sequestration. At this time, although Count Ferraud was a councillor of state, and a permanent under-secretary, he considered his position as merely the start of his political fortune. Preoccupied by the cares of an all-devouring ambition, he had taken on as secretary a ruined ex-solicitor named Delbecq – a man who was more than merely skilful, and knew all the twists and turns of the law inside out – to whom he entrusted the management of his private business. The cunning lawyer, realising the advantages of his position working for the Count, decided that a display of honesty was the best policy so far as his own future gain was concerned. He hoped to rise to a high position by the credit of his employer, whose fortune was the object of his diligence. His behaviour was in such contrast to his previous life that he appeared as the victim of slander. With the tact and the subtle grasp of the situation that more or less all women are endowed with, the Countess, who had guessed at the intentions of her steward, kept a close eye on him, and was able to handle him so adroitly that she had already managed to wheedle him into increasing her own private fortune. She had managed to persuade Delbecq that Monsieur Ferraud was at her beck and call, and had promised to have him appointed president of a Court of First Hearing in one of the biggest towns in France, if he were to dedicate himself entirely to her interests. The promise of a permanent post that would enable him to make a good marriage and to conquer, later on, a lofty position in politics by becoming a *député*, made Delbecq the Countess' henchman. He had not let her miss a single one of the favourable opportunities that the movements of the Stock Exchange and the rise in property prices presented to those in Paris clever enough to profit from them during the first three years of the Restoration. He had trebled his patroness' capital, all the more easily since any means had seemed good to the Countess if she could thereby make a huge fortune on the quick. She used the emoluments of the posts occupied by the Count on her domestic expenses, so as to capitalise her revenue, and Delbecq lent himself to the arithmetic behind this avarice without seeking to understand the reasons for it. Those sorts of people only bother about secrets which their own interests make it imperative for them to discover. Furthermore, he found it natural to explain it by that thirst for gold which affects most Parisian ladies, and such a vast fortune was required to sustain the pretentions of Count Ferraud that the steward sometimes thought he could detect in the avidity of the Countess an effect of her devotion for the man she was still in love with. The Countess had buried the secrets of her behaviour in her innermost heart. That was where the life-and-death secrets involving her were concealed; that was where the knot of this story was tied. At the start of 1818, the Restoration was firmly settled on its apparently unshakeable foundations, and its doctrines of government, as understood by those of superior intelligence, seemed to them inevitably to bring in their wake an era of new prosperity for France; and Paris society changed its face. Countess Ferraud found that she had contracted, quite by chance, a marriage of love, wealth and ambition at one and the same time. She was still young and beautiful, played the part of a fashionable woman, and flourished in the atmosphere at Court. Rich in her own name, and rich through her husband, who, lauded to the skies as one of the most capable men in the royalist party and a personal friend of the King, seemed destined for a ministry, she belonged to the aristocracy and shared its splendours. But amid this triumph, she fell victim to a moral cancer. There are feelings that women can guess at however carefully men try to repress them. When the King had first returned, Count Ferraud started to entertain a few regrets about his marriage. Colonel Chabert's widow had brought him no new allies through marriage, he was alone and without anyone to support him or guide him in a career full of pitfalls and enemies. And then, perhaps, when he had managed to weigh up his wife more coolly, he had realised some of the shortcomings in her upbringing that made her less able to back him up in his plans. A few words he uttered on the marriage of Talleyrand opened the eyes of the Countess, to whom it was now evident that if her marriage had still to be arranged, she would never have become Madame Ferraud. What woman could ever forgive a regret like that? Doesn't it contain in a nutshell every insult, every crime, every rejection? But what a wound those words must have opened in the Countess' heart if we accept the supposition that she was afraid she might see her first husband return! She had known he was alive and she had rejected him. Then, during the period in which she had heard nothing more of him, she had indulged in the idea that he must have been killed at Waterloo, fighting for the imperial eagles in the company of Boutin. Nonetheless she decided to tie the Count to her by the strongest of bonds, a golden chain: and she wanted to be so rich that her fortune would ensure her second marriage was indissoluble, if by chance Count Chabert should reappear. And he *had* reappeared, without her being able to understand why the struggle she dreaded had not already begun. Suffering and illness had perhaps delivered her from that man. Perhaps he was half mad; Charenton might still take care of him for her. She hadn't wanted to take Delbecq or the police into her confidence, for fear of becoming dependent on anyone, or hastening the catastrophe. There are in Paris many women who, like Countess Ferraud, live with a moral monster unknown to the world at large in their heart, or skirt the very verge of the abyss; they grow a thick skin where their conscience pricks them, and still manage to laugh and enjoy themselves.

'There is something really quite odd in Count Ferraud's situation,' Derville said to himself when he emerged from his long reverie, as his cabriolet drew up in the rue de Varennes, outside the gate of the Ferraud residence. 'How can it be that he, so rich and such a favourite of the King, is still not a peer of the realm? It's true perhaps that the King has political considerations in mind, as Madame de Grandlieu was telling me, and wants to highlight the importance of the peerage by not giving it away to all and sundry. In any case, the son of a councillor in Parliament is neither a Crillon, nor a Rohan[13]. Count Ferraud can enter the upper chamber only by stealth. But if his marriage were annulled, couldn't he pick up the peerage of one of those old senators who have only daughters and no sons – to the King's great satisfaction? To be sure, that's a fine story to regale the Countess with and put the wind up her,' he thought as he climbed the steps.

Without knowing it, Derville had put his finger on Madame Ferraud's secret wound and thrust his hand into the cancer that was eating away at her. He was received by her in an attractive winter dining-room, where she was having lunch while playing with a monkey tied by a chain to a kind of little stake adorned with iron rods. The Countess was wrapped in an elegant dressing-gown, and her curls, pinned up casually, fell forward from her bonnet, giving her a mischievous appearance. She was fresh and merry. Silver, vermilion, and mother-of-pearl utensils glittered on the table, and all around her were exotic flowers arranged in magnificent china vases. Seeing the wife of Colonel Chabert, rich with his spoils, in the lap of luxury, at the pinnacle of society, while the unhappy man himself was living in the home of a poor dairyman among the farmyard animals, the solicitor said to himself: 'The moral of this is that a pretty woman will always refuse to recognise her husband, or even her lover, in the shape of a man in an old greatcoat, wearing a couch-grass wig and leaky boots.' A malicious and bitter smile expressed the half-philosophical, half-satirical ideas that were bound to occur to a man so well placed as to see through to the bottom of things, in spite of the lies beneath which most Parisian families hide their existence.

'Good day, Monsieur Derville,' she said, continuing to let the monkey sip her coffee.

'Madame,' he said brusquely, shocked at the frivolous tone of voice with which she had said 'Good day, Monsieur Derville' to him; 'Madame, I have come to talk to you about a rather serious matter.'

'I am so *dreadfully* sorry, the Count is not at home…'

'And I am highly delighted, Madame. It would be a *dreadful* nuisance if he were to be present at our conversation. In any case, I know from Delbecq that you like to conduct your business yourself, without bothering the Count.'

'In that case I'll call Delbecq,' she said.

'He would be no use to you, for all his cleverness,' replied Derville. 'Listen, Madame, a single word will be enough to make you take things seriously. Count Chabert is alive.'

'Do you think you'll get me to take things seriously by uttering such silly nonsense?' she said, with a shrill peal of laughter.

But the Countess was suddenly abashed by the strange lucidity of the questioning gaze with which Derville fixed her, as if he could read into the depths of her soul.

'Madame,' he retorted with a cold and piercing gravity, 'you are unaware of the extent of the dangers that threaten you. I won't mention the incontestable authenticity of the documents, nor the certainty furnished by the proof attesting to the existence of Count Chabert. I'm not the kind of man who will take on a bad case, as you well know. If you oppose our disputing the validity of the death certificate, you will lose this first case, and once this question is resolved in our favour, we're sure to win all the others.'

'So what *have* you come to tell me about?'

'Neither about the Colonel, nor about yourself. Nor will I talk to you about the statements that solicitors with their wits about them could draw up once they were armed with the curious facts of this case, or the profit they would draw from the letters you received from your first husband before celebrating marriage with your second.'

'That is not true!' she said, with all the violence of a young woman of fashion. 'I never received any letter from Count Chabert; and if anyone claims to be the Colonel, it can only be some schemer, some freed convict, like Cogniard, perhaps[14]. It sends a shiver up my spine merely to think about it. Can the Colonel rise from the dead, Monsieur? Bonaparte sent his condolences to me via an aide-de-camp, and I still receive a widow's pension of three thousand francs, granted by Parliament. I was right a thousand times over to turn away all the Chaberts who came along, just as I will turn away those who come along in future.'

'Fortunately, we are alone, Madame. We can lie to our hearts' content,' he said coldly, taking pleasure in goading the Countess to wrath so he could drag a few indiscreet remarks from her. This is a manoeuvre familiar to solicitors, used as they are to remain calm even when their opponents or their clients lose their temper.

'Very well! It's between the two of us,' he said to himself, as he suddenly imagined a trap into which he could lure her and thus demonstrate her weakness. 'The proof of the delivery of the first letter exists, Madame,' he continued aloud, 'it contained money…'

'Money? It did *not* contain any money.'

'So you *did* receive that first letter!' said Derville, with a smile. 'You've already fallen into the first trap set by a solicitor, and you think you can fight against justice…'

The Countess turned red, then white, and then hid her face in her hands. Then she shook off her shame, and resumed with the cold composure natural to that sort of woman, 'Since you are the so-called Chabert's solicitor, do me the pleasure of –'

'Madame,' Derville interrupted her, 'right now I am still *your* solicitor just as much as the Colonel's. Do you think I'm prepared to lose such precious clients as you? But you're not listening to me…'

'Go ahead, Monsieur,' she said, graciously.

'Your fortune came to you from Count Chabert and you turned him away. Your fortune is colossal, and you are leaving him to beg. Madame, solicitors are capable of great eloquence when the cases speak so eloquently for themselves, and here there is a combination of circumstances that could rouse public opinion against you.'

'But Monsieur,' said the Countess, irritated at the way Derville was giving her such a slow and prolonged roasting, 'even if we admit that your Monsieur Chabert really exists, the courts will uphold my second marriage because of the children, and I will get off with letting Monsieur Chabert have his two hundred and twenty-five thousand francs.'

'Madame, we don't yet know which way the courts will incline when it comes to the question of sentiment. If we have, on the one hand, a mother and her children, we also have, on the other, a man overwhelmed by misfortune, and you and your refusals have added years to his age. Where's he going to find a wife? And then, can judges go against the law? Your marriage with the Colonel has right and priority on its side. But if they make you out to be a spiteful person, you might end up with an adversary you are not expecting. That, Madame, is the danger from which I would like to protect you.'

'A new adversary?' she said. 'Who?'

'Count Ferraud, Madame.'

'Monsieur Ferraud feels too much affection for me, and too much respect for the mother of his children –'

'Don't talk such nonsense,' Derville interrupted her, 'to a solicitor accustomed to seeing into the depths of people's hearts. At the moment, Monsieur Ferraud doesn't have the slightest inclination to break up your marriage, and I'm convinced he adores you; but if someone were to come along and tell him that his marriage might be annulled, that his wife will be arraigned as a criminal and treated as a pariah by public opinion…'

'He would defend me, Monsieur!'

'No, Madame.'

'What reason would he have for abandoning me, Monsieur?'

'That of marrying the only daughter of a peer of the realm, whose peerage would be transmitted to him by royal decree…'

The Countess turned pale.

'There!' said Derville to himself. 'Now I've got you: the poor Colonel's case is won.'

'Furthermore, Madame,' he continued aloud, 'he would be all the less prone to remorse in that a man covered with glory, a general, a count, a Grand Officer of the Legion of Honour, could hardly be considered as a second best; and if that man asks him for his wife back –'

'Enough, Monsieur, enough!' she said. 'I'll never have another solicitor but you. What should I do?'

'Compromise!' said Derville.

'Does he still love me?' she said.

'I can't imagine that he doesn't.'

At these words, the Countess lifted her head. A gleam of hope shone in her eyes; she was perhaps thinking she could speculate on the affection of her first husband to win her case by some feminine wile.

'I will await your orders, Madame, to discover whether we are to serve notice of our intentions to you, or whether you wish to come and see me and settle the basis for a compromise,' said Derville, bowing to the Countess as he left.

Eight days after Derville's two visits, one fine June morning, the husband and wife, their union sundered by an almost supernatural chance, left from the most diametrically distant points of Paris to make their way to a meeting in the office of the solicitor they shared. The money generously loaned by Derville to Colonel Chabert had enabled him to dress in a manner befitting his rank. So the dead man was conveyed to his destination in a nice clean cabriolet. He was wearing on his head a wig appropriate to his physiognomy, he was dressed in blue cloth and white linen, and was wearing beneath his waistcoat the red saltire cross of the Grand Officers of the Legion of Honour. Now that he had resumed the habits of a wealthy lifestyle, he had regained his former martial elegance. He was standing erect. His face, grave and mysterious, on which were depicted happiness and all its associated hopes, seemed younger and fuller, to borrow from painting one of its most picturesque expressions. He no longer resembled the Chabert who had gone around in an old greatcoat any more than an old sou resembles a newly minted forty-franc coin. Seeing him, passers-by would easily have recognised one of those fine pieces of debris left over from our bygone army, one of those heroic men who reflect our national glory, and who represent that glory in the same way that a sliver of ice lit up by the sun seems to reflect all its rays. Those old soldiers are, at one and the same time, pictures and books. When the Count emerged from his vehicle to climb the stairs to Derville's office, he leapt nimbly down like a young man. Hardly had his cabriolet turned round when a fine coupé emblazoned with a coat of arms arrived. Countess Ferraud got out, in a costume that was simple but skilfully calculated to show off the youthfulness of her figure. She was wearing a pretty, pink-lined bonnet that framed her face perfectly, concealing its outline and making it look more full of life. But if the clients were now rejuvenated, the office had remained exactly as it was, and presented the same appearance as it did in the description with which this story began. Simonnin was having lunch, his shoulder leaning against the open window; and he was gazing at the blue sky that stretched above the courtyard surrounded by four dark blocks of buildings.

'Ha!' exclaimed the junior clerk, 'who wants to wager tickets to a show that the Colonel is a general, with a red ribbon to boot?'

'The boss really can perform miracles!' said Godeschal.

'So we can't play any tricks on him this time?' asked Desroches.

'It's his wife who's taken on the job – Countess Ferraud!' said Boucard.

'Oh come now,' said Godeschal, 'do you mean the Countess

Ferraud is obliged to be the wife of two –'

'There she is!' said Simonnin.

At this moment, the Colonel came in and asked for Derville.

'He's in, Monsieur le Comte,' replied Simonnin.

'So you're not deaf after all, you little scamp!' said Chabert, taking the errand-boy by the ear and twisting it to the great satisfaction of the clerks, who burst out laughing and looked at the Colonel with the curiosity and consideration owed to that strange personage.

Count Chabert had already gone into Derville's study when his wife came into the main office door.

'I say, Boucard, there's going to be an extraordinary scene in the boss's study! There's a woman who can spend even days at Count Ferraud's and odd days at Count Chabert's.'

'In leap years,' said Godeschal, 'the *count* will be even.'

'Do be quiet, gentleman! They can hear,' said Boucard, severely. 'I've never seen a law firm where people joked so much about their clients as you do.'

Derville had stowed the Colonel away in his bedroom when the Countess presented herself.

'Madame,' he said to her, 'not knowing whether you would find it agreeable to see Count Chabert, I have kept you apart. But if you wish…'

'Monsieur, it's very thoughtful of you. Thank you.'

'I've prepared the original of a document the conditions of which can be discussed by you and Monsieur Chabert forthwith. I will go alternately between you and him, to present you both with your respective demands.'

'Yes, yes, Monsieur,' said the Countess, with an involuntary gesture of impatience.

Derville read aloud:

'*Between the undersigned,*

    Monsieur Hyacinthe, called Chabert, *Count, Brigadier and Grand Officer of the Legion of Honour, living at Paris in the rue du Petit-Banquier, in the first instance;*

    And Madame Rose Chapotel, wife of the aforesaid Count Chabert, née –'

'Go on,' she said, 'let's leave out the preliminaries and come to the conditions.'

'Madame,' said the solicitor, 'the preamble explains succinctly the position in which you both find yourselves. Then, in article one, you acknowledge, in the presence of three witnesses – namely two notaries and the dairyman at whose house your husband has been living, to whom I have confided your business under terms of secrecy, and who will preserve the most complete confidentiality – you acknowledge, as I was saying, that the individual designated in the documents relating to the private agreement – the validity of which is also confirmed by an identity certificate prepared by your notary Alexandre Crottat – is Count Chabert, your first husband. In article two, Count Chabert, in the interests of your happiness, agrees to avail himself of his rights only in the cases laid down in the deed itself. – And these cases,' said Derville parenthetically, as it were, 'are none other than the non-performance of the clauses of this secret agreement. On his side,' he resumed, 'Monsieur Chabert consents to pursue by mutual agreement with you a judgement that will annul his death certificate and declare that his marriage is dissolved.'

'Those aren't at all the terms I wanted,' said the Countess in astonishment. 'I don't want to have a lawsuit on my hands. You know why.'

'In article three,' continued the solicitor, with imperturbable composure, 'you agree to provide Hyacinthe, Count Chabert, with a life annuity of twenty-four thousand francs, registered in the Great Book of the Public Debt, but the capital of which will fall to you on his death…'

'But that's much too much money,' said the Countess.

'Can you argue him down?'

'Perhaps.'

'So what exactly do you want, Madame?'

'I want, I don't want a lawsuit, I want –'

'You want him to stay dead,' Derville broke in emphatically.

'Monsieur,' said the Countess, 'if we need to give him an annuity of twenty-four thousand livres, we'll go to Court –'

'Yes, we'll go to Court,' exclaimed hoarsely the Colonel, opening the door and appearing suddenly in front of his wife, with one hand placed over his stomach underneath his waistcoat and the other pointing to the parquet floor, a gesture which the memory of his adventure made all the more terrible and dramatic.

'It's him,' the Countess said to herself.

'Too much money?' the old soldier continued. 'I gave you nearly a million, and you are haggling over my misfortune. Very well: now I want both you and your fortune. We hold our property in common, our marriage is still in force –'

'But this gentleman is not Count Chabert!' exclaimed the Countess, with feigned surprise.

'Oh?' said the old man, with a tone of the deepest irony. 'Do you need proof? I picked you up at the Palais-Royal…[15]'

The Countess turned pale. Seeing her turn pale beneath her rouge, the old soldier, touched by the intense suffering he was imposing on a woman he had once so ardently loved, stopped; but she darted such a venomous glance at him that he suddenly resumed: 'You were part of the establishment of –'

'I beg you, Monsieur,' the Countess said to the solicitor, 'please excuse me if I leave the room. I didn't come here to listen to such vile insinuations.'

She rose to her feet, and went out. Derville sprang into the main office. The Countess had, as it were, sprouted wings and flown away. Returning into his private office, the solicitor found the Colonel overwhelmed by violent rage, striding up and down.

'In those days, everyone picked up a wife where he could,' he said, 'but I was wrong to choose her, I was taken in by appearances. She is quite heartless.'

'Well, Colonel – wasn't I right to ask you not to come? Now I am certain of your identity. When you made your appearance, the Countess' reaction could only mean one thing. But you've lost your case, your wife knows that no one will recognise you!'

'I'll kill her…'

'That would be crazy! You'd be seized and guillotined like any other wretch. In any case, your shot might miss her: that would be unpardonable, you should never miss your wife when you want to kill her. Let me repair the silly damage you've gone and caused, you great booby! You must be gone. Watch yourself: she's capable of making you fall into a trap and getting you locked up at Charenton. I'll give her notice of our intentions so as to safeguard you from all surprise.'

The poor Colonel obeyed his young benefactor, and left stammering his apologies. He slowly descended the steps of the dark stairwell, lost in his gloomy thoughts, perhaps overwhelmed by the blow he had just suffered, the cruellest blow, the one that pierced him most deeply to his heart – when he heard, as he reached the lowest landing, the rustle of a dress, and his wife appeared.

'Come, Monsieur,' she said, taking his arm with a gesture similar to those that had once been familiar to him.

The Countess' action, and her tone of voice which had become gracious again, were enough to calm the Colonel's anger, and he allowed himself to be led to the carriage.

'Well, up you go!' the Countess told him, when the valet had finished letting down the step.

And he found himself, as if by enchantment, sitting next to his wife in the coupé.

'Where does Madame wish to go?' asked the valet.

'Groslay,' she said.

The horses set off and crossed the entire breadth of Paris.

'Monsieur!' said the Countess to the Colonel, in a voice whose sound revealed one of those emotions that are rare in life, and cause us complete inner agitation.

At times like this, one's heart, fibres, nerves, physiognomy, body and soul – everything shudders, every last pore in one's skin. Life seems to abandon us; it leaves our bodies and gushes forth, spreading like a contagious illness, transmitting itself through our eyes, the accent of our voice, and the gestures we make, and imposes its will on others. The old soldier shuddered on hearing this single word, this first, terrible word: 'Monsieur!' But it was at one and the same time a reproach, a prayer, a pardon, a hope, a despair, a question, an answer. This one word said it all. You had to be an actress to put so much eloquence and so much varied feeling into a single word. Truth never expresses itself so completely; it doesn't show everything on the outside, it leaves you to guess at what lies within. The Colonel was overwhelmed by remorse for his suspicions, his demands, and his anger, and he lowered his eyes so as not to give away the state he was in.

'Monsieur,' continued the Countess, after an imperceptible pause, 'I *did* recognise you.'

'Rosine,' said the old soldier, 'those words contain the sole balm that can help me forget my misfortunes.'

Two round tears rolled hotly onto his wife's hands, which he squeezed in an expression of paternal affection.

'Monsieur,' she continued, 'how could you fail to guess that it cost me a huge effort to appear in front of a stranger in a position as false as is mine! If I have to blush for my situation, let it at least be only among family members. Shouldn't this secret have remained buried in our hearts? You will absolve me, I hope, for my apparent indifference towards the misfortunes of a Chabert whose existence I could hardly be expected to believe in. I received your letters,' she said hurriedly, seeing the objection forming on the features of her husband's face, 'but they only reached me thirteen months after the Battle of Eylau; they'd been opened and soiled, the writing on them was unrecognisable, and I was forced to conclude, once I had obtained Napoleon's signature on my new marriage contract, that some clever schemer was trying to take advantage of me. So as not to disturb the peace of mind of Count Ferraud, and not to affect family relations adversely, I therefore had to take precautions against a false Chabert. Tell me, wasn't I right to do so?'

'Yes, my dear, you were right, and I'm the one who is a stupid creature, a beast, not to have realised I ought to reckon on the consequences of such a situation. But where are we heading?' said the Colonel, seeing that they had reached the city gates at La Chapelle.

'To my country estate, near Groslay, in the valley of Montmorency. There, Monsieur, we will reflect together on the decision we have to make. I know my duties. If I belong to you by right, I no longer belong to you in fact. Can you want us to become the talk of all Paris? Let's not tell the public about this situation, a pretty ridiculous one as far as I am concerned, and let's try and maintain our dignity. You still love me,' she continued, gazing at the Colonel with a sad, sweet expression; 'but wasn't I quite within my rights to form other ties of affection? In this unusual situation, an inner voice tells me I can count on your kindness, as so often in the past. So would I be wrong to take you as the single, sole arbiter of my fate? Be the judge in your own case. I can rely on the nobility of your character. You will be generous enough to forgive me for the results of my innocent misdeeds. So I will confess to you that I love Monsieur Ferraud. I thought there was nothing wrong in loving him. I will not blush at the confession I am making to you; if it offends you, at least it does not dishonour you. I can't hide the facts from you. When chance left me a widow, I was not yet a mother.'

The Colonel motioned his wife to be quiet, and they sat without uttering a single word for half a league. Chabert imagined he could see the two children before his eyes.

'Rosine!'

'Monsieur?'

'Are the dead entirely wrong to return, then?'

'Oh no, Monsieur, not at all! Don't think me ungrateful. But you find a lover and a mother where you had left behind a wife. If it is no longer within my power to love you, I know how very much I owe you and can still offer you all the affection of a daughter.'

'Rosine,' continued the old man in a gentle voice, 'I don't feel any resentment against you. We'll forget everything,' he added, with one of those smiles whose grace always reflects a sensitive soul. 'I am not quite so lacking in delicacy as to demand a semblance of love in a woman who no longer does love.'

The Countess darted a glance imbued with such gratitude at him that poor Chabert wished he had stayed in the common grave at Eylau. Certain men have souls strong enough for such devotion; its reward consists, as far as they are concerned, in the certainty of having caused the happiness of a beloved person.

'My friend, we'll have a quiet talk about all this later, when we've calmed down,' said the Countess.

The conversation took another direction, for it was impossible to continue for long on this topic. Although husband and wife continued to refer frequently to their bizarre situation, either in brief allusions or more seriously, they enjoyed a charming journey, recalling the events of their past union and the days of Empire. The Countess managed to imbue these memories with a gentle charm, and shed over the conversation a hue of melancholy necessary to maintain a fitting gravity. She rekindled love without arousing desire, and gave her first husband a glimpse of all the moral riches she had acquired, trying to accustom him to the idea of restricting his happiness to nothing more than the pleasures a father can enjoy in the company of a beloved daughter. The Colonel had known his wife as a countess in the days of the Empire, now he saw her as a countess of the Restoration. Finally the couple drove along a side road and arrived in extensive grounds situated in the little valley that separates the heights of Margency from the pretty village of Groslay. The Countess owned there a delightful house where the Colonel saw, on arrival, all the preparations that had been made necessary by his stay and his wife's. Unhappiness is a kind of talisman whose power consists in strengthening our original constitution: it increases mistrust and wickedness in certain men, just as it increases the goodness of those who have kind hearts. Misfortune had made the Colonel even more ready to help, and even kinder than he had been, and so he could be initiated into the secret of feminine sufferings that are unknown to the vast majority of men. Nonetheless, despite his lack of mistrust, he could not stop himself from saying to his wife: 'So you were sure you'd be bringing me here?'

'Yes,' she replied, 'if I found that the litigant really was Colonel Chabert.'

The appearance of truthfulness she managed to give this answer made the slight suspicions that the Colonel had (to his shame) harboured evaporate. For three days the Countess was admirable company for her first husband. By her tender care and her constant gentleness she seemed to be intent on effacing the memory of the sufferings he had endured, and gaining forgiveness for the unhappiness which, by her own confession, she had innocently caused; she took pleasure in deploying for him all the charms to which she knew he was partial, while at the same time behaving towards him with a certain melancholy: for we are more particularly susceptible to certain kinds of attention, a certain gracefulness of heart or mind, which we cannot resist; she wanted to engage his interest in her situation, and soften his heart enough to vanquish his mind and have him completely at her beck and call. Resolved to do everything in her power to achieve her aims, she still did not know quite what to do with this man: but she certainly *did* want to destroy him socially. On the evening of the third day she sensed that, for all her efforts, she could not conceal the anxieties that the result of her manoeuvres was causing her. Seeking a moment's relaxation, she went up to her room, sat at her secretaire, dropped the mask of serenity that she kept up whenever she was with Count Chabert, like an actress who, returning exhausted to her dressing room after a demanding fifth act, falls half-dead with fatigue, leaving behind in the auditorium an image of herself which she no longer resembles. She started to finish a letter she had begun to Delbecq, telling him, in her name, to ask Derville for the documents concerning Colonel Chabert, so he could copy them and straight away come to see her at Groslay. Hardly had she finished when she heard in the corridor the steps of the Colonel who, in a state of great anxiety, had come looking for her.

'Ah!' she exclaimed, 'I wish I was dead! My situation is intolerable…'

'Why? What's the matter with you?' asked the old fellow.

'Nothing, nothing,' she said.

She rose to her feet, left the Colonel and went down to speak in private to her chambermaid, whom she sent off to Paris, telling her to put the letter she had just written to Delbecq into his hands personally and to bring it back to her as soon as he had read it. Then the Countess went to sit on a bench where she was visible enough for the Colonel to come and find her as soon as he wanted to. The Colonel, who was already looking for his wife, ran down and sat next to her.

'Rosine,' he said, 'what's the matter?'

She did not answer. The evening was one of those calm and magnificent evenings whose secret harmonies imbue June sunsets with so much gentle beauty. The air was pure and the silence deep, so that from the other side of the grounds could be heard the voices of children adding a sort of melody to the sublimity of the landscape.

'Why won't you tell me?' the Colonel asked his wife.

'My husband…' said the Countess, and then stopped, shrugged, and paused to ask him, blushing, 'What name am I to give Count Ferraud?'

'Call him your husband, my poor child,' replied the Colonel in a kindly voice, 'isn't he the father of your children?'

'Well anyway,' she continued, 'if he asks what I've come here for, if he learns I've shut myself away with a stranger, what will I tell him? Listen, Monsieur,' she said, striking a pose full of dignity, 'decide my fate, I am resigned to anything…'

'My dear,' said the Colonel, seizing his wife's hands, 'I have resolved to sacrifice myself entirely to your happiness –'

'That's impossible,' she cried, with a convulsive shudder. 'Think what you're saying; you'd have to renounce your identity, by signing an official paper –'

'What?' said the Colonel, 'you mean my word isn't enough for you?'

The word *official* pierced the Colonel to the heart and awoke an involuntary sense of mistrust. He turned on his wife a gaze that made her blush; she lowered her eyes, and he was afraid he would find himself obliged to despise her. The Countess feared she had ruffled the unsophisticated modesty and severe probity of a man whose generous character and untutored virtues were known to her. Although these ideas had cast a few shadows across their brows, harmony was soon re-established between them. And this is how. A child's cry echoed in the distance.

'Jules, leave your sister alone!' cried the Countess.

'Oh, so your children are here?' said the Colonel.

'Yes, but I gave them strict instructions not to bother you.'

The old soldier understood the delicacy and feminine tact behind such a gracious precaution, and took the Countess' hand to kiss it.

'Let them come over,' he said.

The little girl ran up to complain about her brother.

'Mama!'

'Mama!'

'He's the one who –'

'She's the one –'

Both pairs of hands were stretched out towards their mother, and the voices of both children blended together. It was an unexpected and delightful tableau!

'Poor children!' exclaimed the Countess, unable to keep back her tears, 'I will have to leave them; who will the courts award them to? You can't split a mother's heart in two – *I* want them!'

'Are you the one that's making mama cry?' said Jules, looking angrily at the Colonel.

'Be quiet, Jules,' exclaimed his mother, imperiously.

The two children stood there in silence, examining their mother and the stranger with a curiosity impossible to express in words.

'Ah yes,' she continued, 'if I am separated from the Count, let them leave me with my children, and I'll do anything they want…'

It was a decisive turn of phrase and it achieved everything she had hoped from it.

'Yes,' exclaimed the Colonel, as if he were completing a sentence he had started to form in his head, 'I must be buried again. I have already said as much to myself.'

'Can I accept such a sacrifice?' replied the Countess. 'If there are men who have died to save the honour of their mistresses, they have given their lives only once. But in this case you would be giving your life every day! No, no, it's quite impossible. If it were merely a matter of your existence, it would be nothing; but to sign that you are not Colonel Chabert, to admit that you are an impostor, to throw away your honour, to tell a lie at every hour of the day – a man's loyalty cannot go as far as that. Just think! No. If it weren't for my poor children, I would already have flown to the ends of the earth with you…'

'But,' Chabert continued, 'can't I live here, in your little summer-house, like one of your relatives? I'm as worn out as a clapped-out cannon, all I need is a little tobacco and the *Constitutionnel*[16].'

The Countess burst into tears. Between Countess Ferraud and Colonel Chabert, there was a contest as to who could be the most noble, and the soldier emerged the victor. One evening, seeing this mother together with her children, the soldier was seduced by the touching grace of a family portrait, in the countryside, amid shade and silence; he took the decision to stay dead and, no longer bothered by the authenticity of any document, he asked how he should go about ensuring once and for all this family's happiness.

'Do whatever you want!' replied the Countess, 'I tell you that I will have nothing to do with this business. I mustn't.'

Delbecq had arrived a few days previously and, in accordance with the Countess' verbal instructions, the steward had managed to win the trust of the old soldier. So the following morning, Colonel Chabert left with the ex-solicitor for Saint-Leu-Taverny, where Delbecq had got the notary to draw up a deed conceived in such blunt terms that the Colonel swept out of the office on hearing them.

'Hang it all! I'd look a real charmer! Everyone would take me for a forger!' he exclaimed.

'Monsieur,' Delbecq said to him, 'I advise you not to sign too quickly. In your place I'd try and get at least thirty thousand livres a year out of the case, for the Countess would give it.'

Having cast on that accomplished scoundrel the witheringly eloquent glance of the man whose honesty has been insulted, the Colonel fled the field, in prey to a thousand contrary emotions. He relapsed into his earlier mistrust, flew into a rage, and then calmed down again in rapid succession. Finally he entered the grounds of the Groslay estate through a gap in the wall, and slowly made his way to an arbour set under a pavilion overlooking the Saint-Leu road, where he could reflect at his ease. The path was strewn with the kind of yellowish earth sometimes used in place of gravel, and the Countess, who was sitting in the morning room in this pavilion, did not hear the Colonel as she was too absorbed in the success of her case to pay the least attention to the slight noise made by her husband. And the old soldier did not notice his wife above him in the little pavilion.

'Well, Monsieur Delbecq, has he signed?' the Countess asked her steward whom she caught sight of, walking alone along the road, over the top of a hedge lining a ha-ha.

'No, Madame. I don't even know what's become of the chap. The old horse is starting to kick out.'

'In that case, we'll ultimately have to get him locked away in Charenton,' she said, 'since he's now in our power.'

The Colonel, who found he still had enough of the sprightliness of youth to leap over the ha-ha, was standing in front of the steward in the twinkling of an eye, and he dealt him the finest pair of slaps that had ever been received on a lawyer's cheeks.

'That's to show you that old horses can still kick out,' he said.

Once his anger had evaporated, the Colonel no longer felt strong enough to jump across the ditch. The truth had been revealed in all its nakedness. The Countess' words and Delbecq's reply had unveiled the plot to which he was going to fall victim. The care and attention they had lavished on him had been a bait to lure him into a trap. These words were like the drop of some subtle poison which caused the old soldier to experience the return of both his physical and his moral pains. He returned to the pavilion through the gate of the grounds, walking slowly, like a broken man. So there was no peace for him, no truce! From now on it would be necessary to wage with this woman the hateful war Derville had spoken to him about, to launch on a life of lawsuits, sup on gall and drink every morning a cup of bitterness. And then – dreadful thought – where would he find the money necessary to pay the costs of the first stages of the trial? Such a great disgust for life swept across him that if there had been a river nearby, he would have jumped into it, and if he had had pistols with him he would have blown his brains out. Then he relapsed into the uncertain train of ideas that, ever since his conversation with Derville at the dairyman's, had changed his outlook. Finally, reaching the pavilion, he went up into the aerial room whose rose windows offered a view over each of the beautiful prospects of the valley, and here he found his wife sitting in a chair. The Countess was examining the landscape with that calm and immovable countenance, that impenetrable physiognomy that women adopt when they are determined to do whatever is necessary. She wiped her eyes as if she had been shedding tears, and played distractedly with the long pink ribbon on her belt. Nevertheless, despite her apparent self-assurance, she could not restrain an involuntary shiver when she saw her venerable benefactor standing in front of her, his arms folded, his face pale, his brow stern.

'Madame,' he said, having stared at her fixedly for a while and forced her to blush, 'I will not curse you, I despise you. Now I thank the chance event that separated us. I do not even feel any desire for vengeance; I don't love you any more. I want nothing from you. Enjoy your life in peace and quiet: you have my word, which is worth more than the scribblings of all the notaries in Paris. I will never lay claim to the name which I have perhaps given lustre to. From now on I'm just a poor devil called Hyacinthe who merely wants his place in the sun. Farewell…'

The Countess flung herself at the Colonel's feet, and tried to hold him back by grasping his hands: but he repulsed her in disgust, telling her: 'Do not touch me.'

The Countess made a gesture that no words could translate when she heard her husband's footsteps walking away. Then, with the profound perspicacity that extreme wickedness or the fierce egotism of the world can give, she decided she could probably live at peace, trusting to the promise, and the contempt, of that loyal soldier.

Chabert did indeed disappear. The dairyman went bankrupt and got a job driving a cabriolet. Perhaps the Colonel took up some similar profession. Perhaps, like a stone thrown into an abyss, he bounced down from ledge to ledge like a waterfall, to lose himself in the ragged tide of mud that rolls across Paris.

Six months after this event, Derville, who had heard nothing more of either Colonel Chabert or of Countess Ferraud, thought that they must have come to an agreement which the Countess had had drawn up in some other law firm, out of vengeance. So, one morning, he estimated the sums of money lent to the said Chabert, added the costs, and asked Countess Ferraud to request Count Chabert pay back the sum total, presuming as he did that she knew where her first husband could be found.

The very next day, Count Ferraud's steward, recently appointed president of the Court of First Hearing in a big town, wrote to Derville these dreadful words:

Dear Sir,

Countess Ferraud has given me the task of informing you that your client had completely abused the trust you had placed in him, and that the individual who claimed to be Count Chabert has acknowledged that he had assumed a false name without just cause.

I am, Sir, etc.
Delbecq

'My goodness, you certainly come across people who have their heads screwed on the right way. There's nothing sacred for them!' exclaimed Derville. 'You can be human, generous, a philanthropist and a solicitor, and they just take you to the cleaners! This business will have cost me more than two thousand francs.'

Some time after receiving this letter, Derville was looking round the lawcourts for a lawyer he needed to speak to who was pleading a criminal case. Chance so had it that Derville entered Court Six at the very moment the president was sentencing a man named Hyacinthe to two months in gaol as a vagabond, and ordering him to be taken thereafter to the workhouse for beggars at Saint-Denis, a sentence which, in accordance with the jurisprudential habits of the prefects of police, is the equivalent of life imprisonment. At the name Hyacinthe, Derville looked over at the condemned man sitting between two gendarmes in the dock, and recognised, in the person of the man just sentenced, the false Colonel Chabert. The old soldier was calm, motionless, almost absent-minded. In spite of his rags, in spite of the wretchedness etched into his face, his features bore witness to a noble pride. His gaze bore an expression of stoicism that a magistrate should not have failed to recognise; but as soon as a man falls into the hands of justice, he becomes nothing more than a moral being, a question *de jure* or *de facto*, just as to the eyes of statisticians he becomes a mere figure. When the soldier had been taken to the office of the clerk of the Court whence he would be taken away with the batch of vagabonds being sentenced at that moment, Derville used the right enjoyed by all solicitors to go wherever they wish in the lawcourts, followed his man to the office and there gazed at him for a while, together with the curious beggars in whose company he found himself. The antechamber of the clerk of the court's office presented at the time one of those spectacles that unfortunately neither law-makers, nor philanthropists, nor painters, nor writers ever come to study. Like all the laboratories devoted to the ins and outs of law, this ante-chamber is a dark, smelly room, along whose walls runs a wooden bench blackened by the perpetual presence of the wretches who end up at this meeting-place for all the miseries of society, from which none of them is ever quite absent. A poet would say that the sun is too ashamed to shed any light into this awful sewer through which so many misfortunes pass! There is not a single seat on which has not lingered some crime being premeditated or already committed; not a single place in which you might not find a man who, driven to despair by the minor dishonour inflicted on his name by his first misdeed, has not started out on an existence at the end of which there waited the guillotine, or the loud report from a suicide's pistol. All those who fall to earth on the cobble-stones of Paris rebound against these yellow walls, on which a philanthropist, quite devoid of any speculative intentions, could decipher the justification of the numerous suicides complained of by hypocritical writers who are quite unable of lifting a finger to prevent them – a justification that is written in this antechamber as a kind of preface to the dramas of the morgue or those of the Place de Grève[17]. Just now, Colonel Chabert sat amongst these men with vigorous faces, dressed in the horrible uniform of poverty, occasionally falling silent or talking in low voices to one another, as three gendarmes on sentry duty were walking up and down, their sabres rattling on the floor.

'Do you recognise me?' said Derville to the old soldier, going over to stand in front of him.

'Yes, Monsieur,' said Chabert, rising to his feet.

'If you are an honest man,' said Derville in a low voice, 'how could you have failed to honour your debt to me?'

The old soldier blushed as if he had been a young girl accused by her mother of a secret love affair.

'What? You mean Madame Ferraud never paid you?' he cried aloud.

'Paid me?' said Derville. 'She wrote to tell me you were a schemer.'

The Colonel raised his eyes in a sublime gesture of horror and imprecation, as if to call Heaven as witness to this new act of deceit.

'Monsieur,' he said, in a voice calm but broken, 'get the gendarmes to do me the favour of allowing me to go over to the office of the clerk of the court, I will sign you a money order that will certainly be honoured.'

On a word spoken by Derville to the brigadier, he was allowed to take his client into the office, where Hyacinthe wrote a few lines addressed to Countess Ferraud.

'Send that to her address,' said the soldier, 'and you will be reimbursed for your loan and your advance. Believe me, Monsieur, when I say that if I haven't shown you the gratitude I owe you for your kind services, I still feel it, right here,' he said, laying his hand on his heart. 'Yes, my gratitude is here, full and entire. But what can unfortunates do? They love, that's all.'

'But,' said Derville, 'didn't you insist on getting an annuity?'

'Don't talk to me about that!' replied the old soldier. 'You just can't imagine the extent of my contempt for the externals of life that mean so much to most people. I suddenly fell prey to an illness: disgust with humankind. When I think that Napoleon is on St Helena, everything in this world is a matter of indifference to me. I can't be a soldier any more, for my misfortune. Anyway,' he added with a childish gesture, 'it's better to have a certain luxury in one's sentiments than in one's clothes. For my part, I fear the contempt of nobody.'

And the Colonel went back to sit on his bench. Derville left. When he returned to his law office, he sent Godeschal, now second clerk, to Countess Ferraud, who on reading the note he brought immediately had the sum owed to Count Chabert's solicitor paid.

In 1840, towards the end of June, Godeschal, now a solicitor himself, was travelling to Ris in the company of his predecessor Derville. When they reached the avenue that leads from the highway to Bicêtre, they noticed under the elm trees lining the road one of those poor old men, hoary-headed and broken down, who have earned their marshal's baton as beggars, living at Bicêtre in the same way indigent women live at the Salpêtrière.[18] This man, one of the two thousand wretches lodged in the Hospice for the Aged, was sitting on a bollard and seemed to be concentrating his entire intelligence on an operation well known to old men, consisting as it does in drying the tobacco of their handkerchiefs in the sun, so as to prevent them getting bleached, perhaps. This old man had a face which attracted one's sympathy. He was dressed in that robe of reddish cloth that the Hospice gives its guests, a kind of horrible livery.

'I say, Derville,' said Godeschal to his travelling companion, 'have a look at that old man. Doesn't he look like those grotesque characters who come over from Germany[19]? To think he's alive, and maybe even happy!'

Derville raised his lorgnon, scrutinised the poor man, gave an involuntary start and said, 'That old man, my friend, is a whole poem, or, as the romantics would say, a drama. Have you sometimes come across Countess Ferraud?'

'Yes, she's an intelligent woman, quite good company, but a little too devout,' said Godeschal.

'That old inhabitant of Bicêtre is her legitimate husband, Count Chabert, the former colonel; she's doubtless had him placed here. If he is in this hospice instead of living in a town-house, it is simply because he reminded the lovely Countess Ferraud that he had picked her up, like a cab, on the streets. I still remember the tigerish glare she gave him at that moment.'

As this beginning had aroused Godeschal's curiosity, Derville told him the story above. Two days later, on Monday morning, as they returned to Paris, the two men glanced over towards Bicêtre, and Derville suggested going to see Colonel Chabert. Halfway down the avenue, the two friends found, sitting on the stump of a cut-down tree, the old man holding a stick in his hand and amusing himself by drawing lines in the sand. Looking at him more closely, they realised he had just had breakfast somewhere other than in the establishment.

'Hello, Colonel Chabert,' said Derville.

'Not Chabert! Not Chabert! My name is Hyacinthe,' replied the old man. 'I'm not a man, I'm number 164, room 7,' he added, gazing at Derville with timid anxiety, the fear of an old man and a child at once. 'Are you going to see the man condemned to death?' he said, after a moment's silence. '*He* isn't married! He's really happy.'

'Poor man,' said Godeschal. 'Do you want some money to buy tobacco?'

With all the naivety of a young Parisian lad, the Colonel avidly held out his hand to each of the two strangers who gave him a twenty-franc coin; he thanked them with a vacant gaze, saying: 'Fine troopers!' He struck up the pose of a man shouldering arms, pretended to take aim at them, and cried with a smile, 'Fire with both barrels! Long live Napoleon!' And he drew in the air with his walking stick an imaginary arabesque.

'The wound he received was of a kind to make him relapse into childhood,' said Derville.

'Him, in childhood?' exclaimed an old denizen of Bicêtre who was watching them. 'There are days when you don't want to tread on his toes. He has all his wits about him – an old philosopher full of imagination. But today, what do you expect? He's feeling glum. Monsieur, he was already here in 1820. One day, a Prussian officer, whose barouche was climbing up the hill towards Villejuif, came by on foot. The two of us, Hyacinthe and me, were on the side of the road. This officer was walking along with another one, a Russian or some such creature, when the Prussian saw the old chap and – what a laugh! – said to him, "You're an old light infantryman, you must have been at Rossbach."

'"I was too young to be there," came the reply, "but I was old enough to be at Jena[20]." The Prussians certainly skeddadled then – they didn't hang about!'

'What a destiny!' cried Derville. 'He started out from the Foundlings' Hospital and he's ended up in the Hospice for the Aged, having in the interval helped Napoleon to conquer Egypt and Europe... Do you know, my friend,' Derville continued after a pause, 'that there are three types of men in our society – the Priest, the Doctor, and the Lawyer – who are quite unable to view the world with any esteem? They all wear black, perhaps because they are in mourning for all virtues and all illusions. The unhappiest of the three is the solicitor. When a man comes for the priest, he is impelled by repentance, by remorse, by beliefs which make him an object of sympathy, raise him in stature, and give the mediator's soul a certain consolation, so that his task is not without its pleasures: he purifies, he repairs, and he reconciles. But we solicitors, we see the same bad feelings coming into play repeatedly, nothing can improve them, our offices are sewers that can never be swept clean. How many things have I not learnt in the discharging of my duties! I've seen a father dying in an attic, without a penny to his name, abandoned by two daughters to whom he had given an income of forty thousand livres! I've seen wills being burnt. I've seen mothers despoiling their children, husbands stealing from their wives, wives killing their husbands by using the love they had kindled in them to drive them to a state of madness or imbecility so they could live at peace with some lover. I've seen women giving to the child of a first marriage tastes bound to lead to its death so they could bequeath their wealth to a love-child.[21] I can't tell you all that I've seen, for I have witnessed crimes against which justice is impotent. At all events, all the horrendous things that novelists think they are making up always fall short of the truth. Now it's *your* turn to discover all these delightful things; as for me, I'm off to live with my wife out in the country: Paris repels me.'

'I've already seen quite a few such cases at Desroches's office,' replied Godeschal.

NOTES

1. The Grand Châtelet, demolished in 1802, had served as the lawcourts under the *Ancien Régime*.

2. Mme Saqui was a tightrope dancer and acrobat.

3. You did indeed have to pay to see the Pont-Neuf, the oldest bridge in Paris: or at least, you had to pay a toll to cross it.

4. Talma (1763–1826) was a celebrated actor: one of his most famous roles was as Nero in Racine's tragedy *Britannicus*.

5. A lithographic stone was used in nineteenth-century printing processes.

6. The full title of *Victories and Conquests*, a vast compilation published in twenty-nine volumes between 1817 and 1823, was *Victories, Conquests, Disasters, Reverses, and Civil Wars of the French, from 1792 to 1815, by a Society of Soldiers and Men of Letters*.

7. The Hôtel-Dieu is a hospital in central Paris.

8. Charenton is the site of a lunatic asylum, founded in 1641.

9. The monster in question was Napoleon: Crottat is parodying the stereotypical language used by ultra-royalists.

10. These *Bulletins* were propagandistic reports designed to raise morale back in France. The bulletin issued after Eylau commented that after the battle, 'the Emperor spent several hours every day on the battlefield, which presented a horrid spectacle but one made necessary by duty. It required a great deal of labour to bury all the dead.'

11. The column in the Place Vendôme was topped by a statue of Napoleon (though not under Louis XVIII, when the story supposedly takes place).

12. The *Faubourg* Saint-Germain was that part of Left-Bank Paris inhabited by many of the most aristocratic families.

13. The Crillon and Rohan families were among the most ancient of France's aristocratic lineages.

14. Pierre Coignard (Balzac misspells his name) was a convict who escaped in 1805 and married the mistress of an aristocrat whose identity he usurped; he was denounced and arrested in 1819.

15. The Palais-Royal is an elegant *place* in Paris where, in the eighteenth and nineteenth centuries, it was easy to pick up prostitutes.

16. The *Constitutionnel* was a liberal newspaper; its Bonapartist tendencies meant it was in fact banned between 1817 and 1819.

17. The Place de Grève was the site, on the right bank of the Seine, where judicial executions were carried out.

18. Bicêtre was the site of a hospice for the elderly. Salpêtrière was a hospital (and mental hospital) in Paris.

19. Probably a reference to the 'grotesque' characters in the tales of the German writer E.T.A. Hoffmann, much admired by Balzac.

20. The French army was defeated at Rossbach (1757) by Friedrich II of Prussia. The battle of Jena (1806) was one of Napoleon's most spectacular victories.

21. Derville's examples are taken from other stories in Balzac's *Comédie humaine*, the series of which *Colonel Chabert* forms part: Derville here alludes to *Le Père Goriot*, *Ursule Mirouët*, *Gobseck*, *La Muse du département*, and *La Rabouilleuse*.

BIOGRAPHICAL NOTE

Honoré de Balzac was born in Tours in 1799. His father was a state prosecutor in Paris, but was transferred to Tours during the French Revolution due to his political opinions. The family returned to Paris in 1814.

Balzac spent his early years in foster care, and did not excel at school. He went on to study at the Collège de Vendôme and the Sorbonne, before taking up a position in a law office. In 1819 his family were forced to move from Paris for financial reasons. They settled in the small town of Villeparisis where-upon Balzac announced that he wanted to be a writer and returned to Paris. His early works, however, went largely unnoticed. In order to increase his reputation in the literary world, Balzac entered the publishing and printing business, but this enterprise was not a success and left him with heavy debts which were to dog him for the remainder of his life.

Dispirited, Balzac moved to Brittany in search of new inspiration, and in 1829 *Les Chouans* appeared. This was a historical novel in the style of Sir Walter Scott and marked the beginning of his recognition as an writer. Between 1830 and 1832 he published six novelettes entitled *Scènes de la Vie Privée*.

In 1833 he had the idea of linking together his existing writings to form one extensive work encompassing the whole of society. This led to the remarkable *Comédie humaine* – a work of some ninety-one novels, with a cast of in excess of 2000 characters, providing a comprehensive image of the life, habits and customs of the French bourgeoisie. Among the most celebrated works of the *Comédie humaine* are *La Peau de chagrin* (1831), *Les Illusions perdues* (1837–43), *La Rabouilleuse* (1840) and *La Cousine Bette* (1846). Balzac spent fourteen to sixteen hours a day writing in order to fulfill his ambitious plans.

During the later years of his life, Balzac befriended Eveline Hanska, a rich Polish lady, through a series of letters, and then, in 1848, he travelled to Poland to meet her. Despite his failing health, the two were married in 1850, although their marriage was to prove short-lived as Balzac died only three months later, on 18 August, in Paris.

Andrew Brown studied at the University of Cambridge, where he taught French for many years. He now works as a freelance teacher and translator. He is the author of *Roland Barthes: the Figures of Writing* (OUP, 1993) and his translations include Zola's *For a Night of Love*, Gautier's *The Jinx*, Hoffmann's *Mademoiselle de Scudéri*, Gide's *Theseus*, Schiller's *The Ghost-seer*, and *Incest* by the Marquis de Sade, all published by Hesperus Press.

HESPERUS PRESS – 100 PAGES

Hesperus Press, as suggested by the Latin motto, is committed to bringing near what is far – far both in space and time. Works written by the greatest authors, and unjustly neglected or simply little known in the English-speaking world, are made accessible through new translations and a completely fresh editorial approach. Through these short classic works, each around 100 pages in length, the reader will be introduced to the greatest writers from all times and all cultures.

For more information on Hesperus Press, please visit our website: **www.hesperuspress.com**

ET REMOTISSIMA PROPE